SOMETHING IN THE BLOOD

Phillip Messinger

authorHOUSE®

AuthorHouse™ UK
1663 Liberty Drive
Bloomington, IN 47403 USA
www.authorhouse.co.uk
Phone: UK TFN: 0800 0148641 (Toll Free inside the UK)
*   UK Local: 02036 956322 (+44 20 3695 6322 from outside the UK)*

Published by AuthorHouse 02/18/2021

ISBN: 978-1-6655-8578-1 (sc)
ISBN: 978-1-6655-8579-8 (e)

Print information available on the last page.

Any people depicted in stock imagery provided by Getty Images are models, and such images are being used for illustrative purposes only. Certain stock imagery © Getty Images.

This book is printed on acid-free paper.

To my wife, Shirley, and my children, Emily and Stuart, who put up with my years away at sea and my periods of introversion and soul-searching.

To all those who are or have been at sea or in the medical profession, may your path be clear.

To the people of Kauai in the Hawaiian Islands who, on the afternoon of September 11, 1992, experienced the worst hurricane to hit the islands in recent history.

ACKNOWLEDGEMENTS

Some parts of this narrative have been sourced from the *Admiralty Sailing Directions, Pacific Islands Pilot Volume 3* and the *Ship Captain's Medical Guide* (HMSO).

Many thanks to my son, Stuart Messinger, for the design and execution of the front cover.

Grateful thanks to the officers and teaching staff of the training ship HMS *Worcester* who prepared me for a life at sea, and to all those with whom I served and who taught me so much.

It is inevitable that in a truth-based narrative such as this, some people may recognise themselves or others—or think that they do. Thank you all for shaping my life.

THE START OF IT ALL

Fourteen years old, a new life starts.
You're shaking—scared as hell!
Make no mistake, you're nothing here.
You know it—just as well.

You walk onto a polished deck,
the brasswork shining bright.
Goodbye to parents, swallow hard,
and dread the coming night.

Unpack and stow your worldly goods,
smile tentatively too.
And hope the boy you're looking at
is just as scared as you.

A whistle blows—a bosun's call
you'll know to call it soon.
A shout to gather—quickly now!
The caller calls the tune.

'Now listen here—you're very young.
The bottom of the heap!
But worry not—all will come clear.
Now go and get some sleep.'

First night away from home and all
that ever you held dear.
A sleepless mix of tears and noise
unusual to your ear.

The dawn comes up at last,
and daily orders rule your days.
And so it starts—and carries on
and moulds you to its ways.

Where did it go, from then to now?
The time just flew away!
The fear has gone—the memories though
of that enormous day

are with us still, as we recall
that watershed of life.
And how it changed us, boys to men,
And shaped our future lives.

CHAPTER 1

BEGINNINGS

C hris groaned with a mixture of pleasure and pain as the girl walked delicately up his back, kneading and massaging with toes and heels as she went. He had heard about this for months —how 'in Japan' the girls would massage your back by walking on you and would deliver all kinds of undreamed-of delights just for the asking.

'In Japan …' —that was all he seemed to have heard since the letter came appointing him to his first ship—all his elder brother could talk about—all his mother worried about. Now here he was, on his first run ashore, in Yokohama's SSS Turkish Bathhouse. Why Turkish he couldn't understand, but it was where the taxi driver had recommended that they go. Three apprentices, all eager to experience—in their own way—the delights of the Orient after a seemingly long, hard voyage from Europe and home.

He had been in something of a dilemma—with the frantic words of his mother ringing in his ears and all the talk of 'cherry-boy', 'losing your cherry', 'bagging off', and so on from the other apprentices. So, he had thought it through. What harm could come of a visit to a 'respectable' bathhouse for a thoroughly cleansing experience, albeit with some aspects of titillation?

The girl was dressed in a small bikini top and shorts—pale green against her olive skin—with long black hair framing her face and a reserved, aloof politeness as she used her few words of English to ensure that all was well. A mixture of fear instilled by his mother, a reserved shyness and, more relevant, the fact that this was a bona fide bath and massage house and not a euphemism for a brothel, ensured that this would indeed be cleansing, rather than any first indoctrination into the mysterious ways of Eastern women.

———～◯◯◯～———

At midnight when he went on cargo watch, it seemed as if every muscle in his body was damaged beyond repair. Gone was the euphoria which often follows a deep massage—that floating, relaxed feeling of lightness and release. Two hours in his bunk had ensured that his muscles now remembered every sharp toe and heel, every probing finger, and that the occasional clinical approach towards his groin—always rewarded by a polite giggle from the girl and an embarrassing stirring of his young manhood—had remained the stuff of fantasy and frustration. At least he could now give a knowing look and an enigmatic smile when reminiscing with the lads!

Later, in his cabin, he started yet again to reflect on what had brought him to this point—apprentice deck officer in a rather ordinary cargo ship and a career in the merchant navy. As a child he'd wanted to be a doctor, but what was it that had appealed to him about the medical profession, and what had seduced him away from it?

He had never really thought about it too deeply before. Obviously being a doctor had something to do with helping people, caring even, but he knew it hadn't been just this. It was more about order, and problem-solving, and having a clear path to follow—and, perhaps, white coats and pretty nurses.

He'd had several experiences of hospitals, and all of them had left him with a common impression of something just beyond his consciousness. Clean, disinfectant smells and a sense of people knowing what they were doing—a feeling of purpose and direction in a confusing world.

He remembered being rushed into hospital with appendicitis and thinking, despite his tender years and the pain, how cool it was to be in an ambulance with bells ringing and lights flashing. He recalled too how he had gazed at the first nurse he saw in the darkened ward and told her how beautiful she was.

The next nurse he met that night was a West Indian student, and his only-just-teenage heart had fallen in love with her straight away! Was it pubescent lust that had nearly set him on a complete career path? No, this wasn't lust; this was love.

Later in life he would become aware that somewhere, lurking undetected in his subconscious, had been the thought that if he loved her, then she might love him. In fact, that all through his early life he had longed for someone to love him—this despite being in a reasonably loving family. The love he sought had to come from outside that which he had a right to take for granted. Being cared for—nurtured—perhaps gave him a feeling akin to being loved, and if the nurturer seemed to be attracted to him then so much the better.

So, what had caused him to change his mind, that day on the training-ship only a couple of years later? He was visiting his older brother, and he remembered it so clearly—walking up the stairway on the outside of the hull, into the 'half-deck' where everything was polished and orderly, and then a bugle call, shouted orders, people running from all directions and forming into an integrated unit. The smell!—tarry ropes, floor polish, brass-cleaner, and the warm, slightly sweet-rotten smell of the Thames at near-low tide on the ebb. It all added up to—something again on the edge of consciousness—something he needed more than wanted, something to do with purpose, of direction, of being an integral part of something bigger. But also something about himself, about personal identity and image—having something about himself of which to be proud. From that moment he just knew that he had to be in such an environment.

At some time in life, everyone probably has a moment—a split-second lightning flash when things become clear, or they come together to reveal a truth, or the root of a fear, or the solution to a puzzle which has been hanging on the edge of consciousness.

It might be the moment of falling in love, or when the pieces fall into place and a decision makes itself—a path revealed. Only time will tell if it is for the good or not. Sometime later, hindsight may generate a glimpse of another road, a fork in the path which could have been taken—an alternative which may indeed have been taken in another dimension—another universe, but not in this one.

That glimpse may be revealed by wishful thinking; or perhaps circumstances lead us to an opportunity to revisit or review, to imagine ourselves treading that alternative path—'if only I had …' But we'll never know, because we cannot be sure how the uncertainty of future events and the unpredictability of life would have panned out.

Anyway, from that moment nothing would stop him from going to sea. That moment had enticed him away from all thoughts of studying medicine and becoming a doctor.

The training ship was a low-tier public school, set up to train and develop boys for a career in the merchant navy. From a cadet's point of view it was a prison hulk—black and white, three masted, and moored in the Thames a tantalising three hundred yards off the muddy foreshore. From a parent's point of view, it was a pit in which to throw money, with the cost of fees, uniforms, books, and so on but with the reward of seeing their little darling marching, growing, and developing over three years into a man—completely bypassing the stage of unruly teenager into arrogant, young, 'know it all' manhood.

Having survived that and having risen from the ranks of junior dogs-body to that of senior cadet, petty officer, 'leaver', and having the self-image of being the 'dogs-bollocks', in the final term this young man had to persuade a shipping company to employ him as an apprentice.

An apprentice, or cadet—or even midshipman in some companies—was again a junior dogs-body who was there to learn the trade. He (exclusively 'he' at that time) signed an indenture which forbade him from visiting 'taverns, ale-houses, or houses of ill-repute'.

Some joined as trainee pursers or engineers, but those who did so from the training ship only tended to do that if they had failed their eyesight tests. As 'deck apprentices' they were junior officers, somewhere below the non-officer crew members. What they actually did was dependent on the particular shipping company they had joined, and on the attitude and interest of the officers they sailed with. A 'good apprenticeship' provided a blend of bridge time—watch keeping, navigation, and so on—and the manual labour of seamanship and ship maintenance, possibly under a fatherly bo'sun.

Chris had survived—thrived on—all this, and at the end of it he had been offered the position of junior fourth officer. From then on it was sea-time and leave, interspersed with periods of college study and 'Board-of-Trade' examinations, culminating in the award of a 'master mariner's certificate' at the age of 26.

Somewhere though, throughout those thirteen or fourteen years, in the back of his mind he would occasionally wonder about that other path, that un-travelled road, and whether the headstrong rush he'd felt on his initial visit to the training-ship had set him on the right track.

Jonathan awoke to the clamour of the telephone. He stumbled into wakefulness, groping for the phone and trying to clear his head enough to make sense of the incoming information—'men's surgical; post-operative problem; need to hurry; on call, please hurry!' This was the fourth time in three hours, and he'd been on call for sixteen hours already, with eight more to go. Eight hours of trying to make the right decision with not enough information. Eight hours of feeling that people were trying to catch him out, make him feel stupid, overload him to find his breaking point. Not for the first time he found himself thinking, 'Is this what I joined up for? Is this really it? Maybe I should have gone to sea after all.'

His dad had wanted him to go to sea—had dreams of him being the captain of a great liner someday, to achieve what he had not been able to. He was so consistently pushy with this idea that Jonathan had found himself resisting it more and more. After all, just because Dad had developed a heart murmur in his early twenties and couldn't stay at sea, why should he try to live out his dream through his son? And anyway, Mum had rather liked the idea of her son becoming a doctor, so perhaps it was partly to please her that he'd moved in that direction.

Ruefully he thought, 'Mum didn't exactly envisage it being like this. And more to the point, neither did I!' as he struggled back into his creased scrubs, gulped the cold coffee he'd left on the side table, and left for the ward.

With three A levels and good grades, coupled with an outer self-confidence developed through several years at a huge comprehensive school, he had no great difficulty getting a place at university to study medicine. He had gone for the more red-brick establishments, feeling that perhaps 'Oxbridge' and so on would see through his body armour. He was also aware of having to 'big-up' his enthusiasm for a lifelong career in medicine, recognising as he did an appetite for a fast-moving seat-of-the-pants kind of life which was probably achievable as a young doctor but not at a more mature age.

Well, here he was—fast-moving and seat-of-the-pants every minute of every day!

CHAPTER 2

A NIGHT AT THE MOVIES
(EVENING OF WEDNESDAY, 8 SEPTEMBER)

Midweek movie night—mid-Pacific, nothing much about, and it was Wednesday. Dinner was good as the cook had done his special steak-and-kidney pie, and Chris had relaxed his personal rule and had half a bottle of wine with the meal—sharing the bottle with the chief engineer. Now it was time to relax while the lads set up the projector for a showing of James Bond, one of the few movies onboard which most people hadn't seen.

Just as they had got into the story, there was a knock on the smoke-room door, and a rather distraught pumpman staggered in, clutching a plastic bowl. 'Christ, Dave, what's up? You look awful!' said someone. The lights went up and the projector was stopped. Dave muttered something about needing to see the captain and then collapsed on the deck, spilling the contents of the bowl across the carpet. Dark red, congealed into great lumps—blood everywhere.

'What the fuck! Someone get a cloth! Dave, can you hear me?' Chris leaned over the prostrate figure of the pumpman, who was out cold and breathing shallowly, dribbling yet more blood onto his denim shirt. 'Call the chief steward, and tell him to get in here with the *Medical Guide!*'

Like all master mariners, Chris had been trained in first aid and the rudiments of practical medical emergency management. His bible in this regard was the *Ship Captain's Medical Guide*, a book replete with gory photographs and descriptions, diagnostic tools, and descriptions of various treatments—even 'cut along the dotted line' instructions for a few simple surgical procedures, if one could stop one's hands from shaking sufficiently!

Dave started to come to, muttering and swearing but too weak to struggle. 'What happened, Dave? You're throwing up blood, man!'

Dave nodded. 'Second time tonight, Cap; thought it was just a strain at first, but Christ! I'm bloody dying!'

Later Chris was to ruefully remember his very first concern—the smoke-room carpet and the need for a cloth! But his second thought was something like, 'Pumpman, pump rooms, chemicals, cocktail—who knows what awful mixture?' He'd also attended the various courses necessary to have his certificate endorsed for service in chemical tankers—organic chemistry, chemical safety, and so on. Somehow at that moment though, waving those pieces of paper around didn't seem to offer much solace.

'Dave! Have you been working in the pump rooms or been exposed to any cargo fumes today?' Dave shook his head weakly, indicating no, but by this time the chief steward had arrived with the book. 'You're not dying, mate. We've got the book here! Just relax for a bit, and we'll have you OK. You've probably torn something.'

'Bloody alkie!' said the chief steward. 'I've told him and fucking told him that he can't live on whisky, but he's still into a bottle a day and probably not eating anything—are you?—you stupid bastard!'

'I've had the 'flu, haven't I? Haven't felt like eating, but I've been taking the aspirins like you said.'

'Oh, shit!' breathed Chris. 'So let's get this straight. You've been taking aspirin for the flu, not eating, and drinking a bottle of scotch a day—for how long?'

'Three or four days,' said the chief steward, but I told him to eat and to stop the drinking. It's not my bloody fault!'

'Never mind that now. Dave, you've probably got a bleeding ulcer or a tear or something. Been coughing a lot?'

Dave nodded.

'We need to get you into bed and start getting you on the mend. Let's get him into the hospital.'

A couple of the off-duty engineers went to help Dave to his feet, but as they did so he groaned and went a greyish white colour even more than before. Suddenly he vomited a gout of fresh blood across the room.

'Jesus, my fucking new shoes!' shouted the chief steward as he looked down at his ruined white buckskins.

'Serves you bloody right for doling out aspirins to an alcoholic, you twat'—not spoken but thought, as Chris indicated to lower him gently to the deck again.

Taking his pulse revealed a thready beat—fast and light, but at least still going. 'Right boys, let's get him into the hospital as quickly as we can, but try to keep his head below his heart. I think his blood pressure's gone for a burton. Christ, this is serious!'

Once in the hospital and on the high cot, Dave regained consciousness while the chief steward and the captain cleaned him up a bit.

Chris had already called for the radio officer to come down, so he stepped out of the small, one-bed cell with its cupboards and antiseptic smells and started quizzing 'Sparks'. He knew that they were around dead-centre between Hawaii and the US mainland, so there was no point in doing anything dramatic with the ship for the moment. She was riding easily to the long ocean swell and making about 90 per cent of her absolute maximum speed.

Chris and Sparks knew that their best bet was to contact the US Coast Guard. The medical guide was a bit vague— talked about maintaining blood pressure, getting assistance, but it didn't actually say what to *do*, for Christ's sake.

'What about AMVER?' said Chris.

'Yeah, but I thought that was for the Atlantic.'

'No, it's worldwide—probably started for the Atlantic icebergs but it's the American "Automated Merchant Vessel Reporting System." I logged our voyage with them before we left the Panama—gave it to the agent, so at least they'll know roughly where we are.'

'OK, Skip, I'll try to raise the Coast Guard at San Diego or Hawaii. What d'you want me to tell them?'

'Try to get me in voice contact with them, but tell 'em we've got a possible bleeding ulcer or tear—loads of blood, loss of consciousness, and for God's sake, fucking help! Oh, and see if you can raise a ship in our area with a doctor onboard—passenger ship or a Russian. They often have them.'

He counted himself lucky that he still had a radio officer. Most of his contemporaries had been required to learn all sorts of new stuff to go with the new communications equipment. Radio officers were being phased out, leaving the electrician to master all the electronics and the captain to handle all the automated communications. They'd been upgraded to telex a few years ago, so that replaced most of the dot-dash stuff, but the new sat-coms took a bit of getting used to, and it was so time consuming!

Chris checked on Dave and made sure the chief steward was setting up a constant watch on him, even if he was still more concerned about his shoes. 'Sips of water, Chief— nothing else.'

'D'you want me to knock off the aspirins, Captain?'

'Jesus Christ, *yes*! Of course I do!'

Making his way to the bridge, Chris called in on the chief engineer who was in his office working on fuel and endurance figures. He'd obviously heard the buzz, and he knew what might happen.

'What d'you reckon, Bob?' Chris didn't have to say more.

'Well, we can squeeze another knot and a half out of her if we have to, which will give us, say, two hours shorter passage for each day we have to do it. Cost a lot of fuel, of course, but we're OK for Honolulu or back to the States with a safe margin. We'll have to refuel light diesel though, to make Yokohama after a deviation.'

Up on the bridge the second mate had already been alerted and started to plot possible routes and distances. 'Honolulu is the closest port, Captain, by about a day and a half over San Diego. It'll put days onto our ETA Yokohama as it takes us off the Great Circle and well south of our intended route. Warmer weather though,' he chuckled.

'Yeah, well, we've got to look for the silver lining, haven't we? But have you seen the latest weather maps? Something cooking up down south. Could be the beginnings of a big blow.'

CHAPTER 3

SOLUTIONS
(NIGHT OF WEDNESDAY, 8 SEPTEMBER)

'I've got 'em, Skipper—US Coast Guard on voice SSB—bit crackly though. D'you want it through there?'

'Yes, please, Sparks. Well done, and thanks. Sec, give me the present position etcetera, will you.'

Chris walked to the handset on the bridge-front console and listened.

Excelsior, Excelsior, this is US Coast Guard San Diego. How me? Over.'

'US Coast Guard this is *Excelsior*. Hearing you loud and clear, and boy are we pleased to talk to you. I have a medical emergency. Over.'

After confirming the ship's position at 41 degrees 32 minutes north and 149 degrees 05 minutes west, and other important details, Chris spelled out the nature of the problem, to be told that the US Coast Guard had the ship on its AMVER plot and was getting the duty medical officer to the radio.

'Doesn't look good though, Captain, as you're a long way from any of us, and there's the possibility of a pretty big storm heading your way. The good news though is that there are a couple of ships reasonably close to you, and we're already in the process of contacting them to see if any of them can assist you.'

'Captain!' A white-faced chief steward appears on the bridge. 'I'm not very good with this blood pressure thing, but I don't like the look of him, and his pulse is very weak. I can't actually measure his blood pressure, and he seems to be passing out more often.'

'Oh shit, Chief. Well, just keep him lying down, and we'll get some advice pretty shortly, I think. Just stay with him and try to reassure him that we're getting some help.

Excelsior, US Coast Guard San Diego.' A different voice this time—more of a southern drawl and (imagination?) a sound of confidence as the American started to ask some questions about the 'guy with the problem'.

'Captain, I believe that your man has a bleeding ulcer or a stomach tear—much as you suspected—and we really need to do two things pretty damn quickly. D'you have any "giving sets" onboard?—sterile packs of tubing for administering blood or saline? Over.'

'US Coast Guard, *Excelsior*. I think so. We're a chemical tanker, so we've got loads of stuff for dealing with chemical spills, poisoning, and so on, but for Christ's sake we've not been properly trained to use them in case we kill someone!'

'What we need to do is get some saline into this guy, to stabilise his blood pressure. Then we need to try to stop, or at least control, the bleeding. Saline OK with you? You got plenty of that stuff?'

'Chief—saline?—big plastic bags of clear fluid?'

14

'Well, we've only got old stuff. We use it for eyewash, but I don't think we've got any for squirting into people's veins, for God's sake! I'll get onto it straight away.'

'US Coast Guard, *Excelsior*. Say we have got this stuff, will that fix the problem?'

'Well, we can talk you through filling him up with saline, but we're gonna need more than that—got to control that bleeding or he'll just dilute and bleed out!' Ever heard of gastric lavage?'

Chris had done the courses; he'd even spent a week of evenings in a casualty department a few years ago patching up drunks. What he hadn't done was anything like this— yes, a bit of stitching, and even injecting an orange with distilled water as training for administering drugs intra-muscularly. 'We don't want you going 'round sticking stuff into people's veins and killing them, or opening yourself up to a manslaughter charge now, do we?' said the company doctor who would never, ever, find himself in a breathing apparatus, with a poisoned seaman in the cargo pump room of a chemical tanker, surrounded by a cocktail of God-knows-what lethal stuff, protecting the company's reputation. Or in mid-Pacific with a pumpman who was bleeding to death and didn't look much like an orange!

'Message from the chief steward, Cap. No decent saline—only eye wash, but we've got the giving-sets.'

'OK, Pete, thanks.'

'US Coast Guard, *Excelsior*. No saline, but we're OK for the giving-sets, so what now?'

'*Excelsior*, I want you to talk to our operations guys now. I think we see a plan coming together—just patching you through. I'm the duty doc, and I'll be around, so we'll talk later, OK?'

'Thanks, Doc, standing by.'

'*Excelsior*, this is AMVER co-ordination centre Washington. Am I speaking with the captain? Come back.'

'Affirmative, AMVER Washington, Captain Chris Davis here. Over.'

'OK, Chris—now listen up. You need saline, and we've got plenty. We've also got a great big airplane that can drop it to you! We'd like to drop some of our paramedics to help you out too, but the weather is due to cut up real bad for you soon, and we don't want to delay the saline. According to our plot there's a big ship—one of your British luxury cruise liners—around twenty-four hours from you, and she may be able to offer help if the weather holds. How does that sound? Come back.'

'AMVER Washington, *Excelsior*. That sounds great. Should we turn towards your aircraft, or can we head for the passenger ship? Over.'

'OK, *Excelsior*, our bird can make 460 knots, and she'll come from San Diego, so you're better off to head for a rendezvous with the other ship. I believe she's to your south-west, and we'll come find you as soon as we can—estimate about er, five hours from now. Come back.'

'AMVER Washington, *Excelsior*. Affirmative. Can you give us details of the other ship, please, and we'll let you know our course to meet her and prepare for your airdrop. What sort of plane will it be? Over.'

'*Excelsior*, we'll send a Hercules long-range airplane. You won't miss her! The ship showing on our plot and already preparing to meet you is the *Arcturus*. She's now in position 31 degrees 38 minutes north and 170 degrees 01 minutes west. For the moment, our plot shows you need a course of 240 degrees true at your top speed, and we'll get her to turn towards you. Allowing for your slow-down to pick up the saline, with a closing speed of around 39 knots you should be able to meet up in about twenty-six hours. What's your view of the weather forecast for then? Come back.'

'AMVER Washington, *Excelsior*. We've been watching the storm to our southeast for a few days now. Wouldn't normally worry us, but it looks as if we'll be pretty close to it around then and picking up a hefty swell; we're already feeling it a bit now. Early days though. Let's get going with the plan. How much is it going to cost us? Over.'

'*Excelsior*, AMVER Washington. Our compliments, Chris. We appreciate the bombing practice, and we'd only be doing a drill if we didn't have you! About half-a-million dollars though, all up! Anyhow, the doctors here say they'll have a paramedic onboard the plane who'll talk you through the process with the saline. We'll get the bird in the air to meet you at daylight—around 1345 Zulu, OK? They'll be on VHF channel 6, and they'll want you to make plenty of smoke from about 1330 Zulu. Any problem with that?'

'AMVER Washington, *Excelsior*. Affirmative—smoke from 1330 GMT and VHF 6 for the Hercules. No problem with making smoke! And thanks a full million! Over and out.'

'OK, Cap. Gone me. Out.'

CHAPTER 4

ACTION THIS DAY
(THURSDAY, 9 SEPTEMBER)

Chris checked his wristwatch and with a shock noted that it was just past midnight, or 0800 GMT. He turned to the Second mate. 'OK then, Sec, let's turn to 240 degrees true, and I'll talk to the chief about getting a few more knots out of her.'

'240 degrees true, Captain. Will the extra speed really help much?'

'Well, it'll make everyone feel as if we're doing all we can—add a sense of urgency, as if we needed it! Sparks, can you raise the *Arcturus*? I'll be happier talking to them direct.'

'Can't guarantee voice, Cap, but I'll give 'em a call, and I can always put out a 'Pan Pan' during the silence period. They'll know we're looking for them. I'll get back to you.'

An hour or so later, the ship having increased to maximum revolutions and an extra knot with lots of purposeful vibration, the radio officer advised the captain that he had *Arcturus* on voice. Chris again picked up the bridge handset to hear the voice of the Captain, Colin Jenkins, confirming positions with the radio officer.

'OK, Sparks, thanks. Hello, *Arcturus*, this is Chris Davies, captain of the British chemical tanker *Excelsior*. How d'you hear me? Over.'

'Loud and clear, Captain. Sounds like you need our help. We're all with you including most of the passengers, and we've got a bit of a plan worked out provided the weather allows. Over.'

'*Arcturus*, *Excelsior*. Many thanks. We reckon that if you're already on 060 degrees true at your maximum speed, we could meet up around this time tomorrow. How do you see it? Over.'

'*Excelsior*, *Arcturus*. Confirm that, but if our plan is to work, we'll need to wait for daylight—say around 1430 GMT tomorrow the 10th. Let's just use Zulu Time GMT, as our ship's time may be different to yours. Time now 0920 Zulu. Check?'

'*Arcturus*, *Excelsior*. Check that, Captain—my name's Chris by the way—GMT throughout. We're going to get some saline from the American Coast Guard in a few hours to keep our guy alive. Are you going to give us a doctor? Over.'

'*Excelsior*, *Arcturus*. Well, that's the plan Chris—I'm Colin—if we can heave-to near you, we'll put our "baby doc" onboard with a load of gear, and he'll try to sort your guy out. We can both steam in company for Honolulu afterwards if you need to land your man, and we'll take our doctor back as soon as he's happy and go full speed for Honolulu then, OK? Over.'

'*Arcturus*, *Excelsior*. Well, that sounds great, but the weather may not be on our side by then. We may need to do it all on VHF and the medical guide. Over.'

'*Excelsior*, Arcturus. Yes, we've discussed that, but the docs here are not happy about that option—they say you'll need a hand. Our senior doctor is quite happy to sacrifice Baby Doc if necessary! She says it'll be good for him! Over.'

'*Arcturus*, Excelsior. Well, I hope it won't come to that. By the way, we'd be quite happy to look after your senior doctor! Over.'

'*Excelsior*, Arcturus. No way! She's the best-looking woman on here—youngest too! Anyhow, Baby Doc is fully experienced, and if we can get him onboard you may have to keep him for a while. You go get your saline, and we'll take it from there. By the way, d'you want to talk to Baby Doc about administering the saline? Over.'

'*Arcturus*, Excelsior. What I'd really like is three hours sleep and then a chat with your doctors. Is that OK? Over.'

'*Excelsior*, Arcturus. Fully understand, Chris. We'll listen out for you in three hours from now and have both our doctors ready to talk to you, OK? Over.'

'*Arcturus*, Excelsior. Fine. And thanks, Colin. Over and out.'

'*Excelsior*, Arcturus. Out.'

Chris wearily said to no one in particular, 'Well, our increase in speed is pretty pointless if we're going to meet too early for daylight tomorrow, so I'll go and talk to the chief, and we can ease down again.' He repeated this to the second mate—told him that they'd be slowing right down for the rendezvous with the aircraft—and checked that the bridge team were clear on what to do, when. Then he went below, first to the chief engineer and then to see the patient, who was awake and conscious though still vomiting blood almost on the hour.

'Am I going to be OK, Captain? I'm pretty scared. Am I going to die?'

'Well, Dave, we've got the best of the best on our side, and provided we can get some saline into you and a doctor onboard, I reckon you'll be fine. Try to rest easy, and we'll be giving you some real help in a few hours.'

'OK, Cap, and thanks.' He drifted off into a sort of sleep, watched over by Ramon, the second steward.

Chris couldn't have said what was in his heart; he was asking himself the same question, and he truly didn't know the answer. To be this sick, this far from land and with no real professional assistance to hand, well, it didn't really need saying that the odds were against a good outcome.

He had spent his time at sea on all sorts of ships and had been witness to lots of accidents and illnesses. Passenger ships had doctors onboard and occasionally a ship had to be slowed down to reduce vibration and movement while a delicate emergency procedure was carried out. A flu epidemic onboard one ship had killed seven elderly passengers in a week. The doc reckoned they had all been told by their GP to 'go and have a cruise—it'll be good for you!' They were all buried at sea 'to avoid the paperwork,' and Chris's only role had been to hold the captain's cap and carefully watch any relatives in case they rushed too close to the shipside rail.

Cargo ships and tankers, with no doctor onboard, were often crewed by seamen from the Indian subcontinent or the Far East, and some of those were a bit frail. Several times Chris had been called upon to extract a painful—and luckily quite loose and rotten—tooth from the betel-red mouth of a scared but grateful Lascar, or to immerse a man in an ice-bath to control a raving malarial fever. On one trip as chief officer, his captain had suffered with such dreadful toothache that they had even made plans to divert the ship before he went mad!

Chris had himself had a near-death experience, which he had never forgotten. It was on a new cargo ship on which he was third officer for the maiden voyage. The ship was revolutionary—cranes instead of derricks, automatic covers on the cargo holds, air-conditioned cabins and carpeting on the bridge!

It fell to him to move one of the cranes, which weighed thirty-five tons and which could traverse on rails across the ship to aid access to the holds. With nobody in the cab for safety reasons, big friction-brakes were loosened on the chassis while magnetic safety-brakes held the crane until the electric shifting motors engaged to trundle the whole thing to the desired position.

Only done in port, of course, and always without incident, on this occasion the ship was part loaded and had a few degrees list to starboard. She was leaning over a bit—with the crane on the port, or high side. Chris released the mechanical brakes—one on each side—and approached the control box to move the crane.

As he did so, it started to move of its own accord, and Chris slipped in a pool of hydraulic fluid on the deck, between the approaching crane and its buffers. Thirty-five tons of runaway steel was heading straight for his chest with nothing to stop it. He had screamed—knowing that he was going to die—and then he had slipped farther down, clearing the buffer and sprawling on the deck in front of the chassis. The crane hit the buffer, which sheared off but not before stopping the crane in its tracks.

Chris couldn't believe he was still alive—for that short moment he had known that this was the end—but no. After an enquiry which showed that the crane's magnetic brakes had been wired up the wrong way 'round, and a severe reprimand from the chief marine superintendent for not checking beforehand, he was left to reflect on his experience.

So, he felt he understood something of the pumpman's fears.

As the ship quietened down to her normal sea speed, Chris grabbed a couple of hours of fitful sleep before going back on the bridge. At 0430 ship's time he was on the radio again, talking to the doctors onboard *Arcturus* who gave him clear instructions on preparing the giving-set, finding a vein, and administering the saline drip.

'Your biggest problem is going to be finding a vein. His low blood pressure will mean that they are going to be pretty collapsed and difficult to see, let alone pierce.'

Chris thought he'd worry about that later; for the moment his more immediate problem was that the swell was increasing by the hour, that the barometer was dropping steadily, and that a big bird was apparently going to bomb his ship with little plastic bags of salt water!

Talking to the chief officer on the bridge, it was agreed that they would call all hands and get everyone out on deck with hard hats on to look out for the aircraft and to grab whatever came their way. Both lifeboats were swung out and prepared for immediate launching in case they were needed to retrieve the precious saline, and all available heaving lines were laid out along the deck. The bosun was asked to improvise some additional grappling hooks, which he did with bunches of bent welding rods attached to the heaving lines.

Once everyone was up and doing, Chris broadcast to the whole ship—something he didn't do very often—and told them what was likely to happen. He then talked again to the chief engineer, and just after 0530 ship's time, thick, oily, black smoke started pouring out of the funnel and streaming forward, caught on the brisk wind from astern.

'*Excelsior, Excelsior.* British tanker *Excelsior*, this is US Coast Guard Hercules calling *Excelsior* on channel 6. Did anyone order a pizza? Come back.'

This was the call they had been waiting for, and it galvanised the bridge team. The chief officer immediately grabbed the latest position from the new satellite system and handed it to the captain, who picked up the VHF handset. The chief officer then broadcast to offer a free case of beer to the first person who spotted the aircraft.

'US Coast Guard, *Excelsior*. Loud and clear, steering 240 degrees true at two knots and making smoke. Over.'

'*Excelsior*, US Coast Guard. We have you on our surface radar and will be with you in five minutes, approaching you from the north-east—uh, we think we have you on visual—orange ship, lots of smoke? Come back.'

'US Coast Guard, *Excelsior*. That's us. What's the plan? Over.'

'OK, *Excelsior*, if you could put the wind astern so long as the swell's OK, we'll over-fly you at three hundred feet, then we'll turn and make two runs, one from aft to forward and one from port to starboard. We'll drop a whole load of boxes on drogue chutes. You only need the one! Come back.'

'US Coast Guard, *Excelsior*. Roger that. Standing by. Over.'

A shout from the upper deck—'There she is!' And all eyes turned onto the starboard quarter to see a small, dark shape, rapidly growing larger to reveal a gigantic silver aircraft—four propeller engines leaving a light brown trail behind them and a huge ramp slowly lowering from the rear of the craft.

Almost immediately the plane was past them, dipping her wings rapidly in turn, then turning to port to make a long path away and behind the ship—turning again and purposefully pursuing them, getting lower and larger as she approached.

The VHF radio, by this time on the bridge-wing speakers, burst into life. '*Excelsior*, US Coast Guard. Commencing our first run.' Then almost immediately, 'Load released!' as a dozen bright orange drogue parachutes blossomed in the dull morning light and floated quickly down, to land neatly in the water all around the slowly rolling ship.

'Damn!' said Chris, echoed in much more colourful language by most people on deck. 'Bosun—port-side aft— quick, man!—grapnels!'

Just as an elated seaman managed to snag one of the buoyancy-ringed packages with his heaving-line, the Hercules again roared in—this time from the port beam and looking even lower and larger. An almighty roar, a smell of burned paraffin, and she was past, figures waving from the stern ramp and another blossoming of drogues. Two of them landed right on the deck and were immediately pounced on by small groups of eager hands—as excited as if it were a playground game.

Chief Officer Ted Cummings, on deck by this time and talking to the bridge by VHF handset, took charge of the packages which, miraculously, seemed to have shed their buoyancy collars and drogues by now. He reported the successful recovery of three and had them carried to the hospital where, by now, Chris was waiting for them, feeling a lot more nervous than he looked.

Meanwhile, the radio officer had continued to talk to the Hercules, thanking them profusely and assuring their onboard paramedic that the conversation with him and the doctors onboard *Arcturus* had given his captain both the knowledge and the confidence to do what was necessary with the saline. The Hercules crew confirmed that they would update their base in San Diego and the AMVER control centre in Washington, who would continue to listen and co-ordinate the next phase.

 **CHAPTER 5**

TO SAVE A LIFE

C hris was familiar with the 'giving set'—a clear plastic tube arrangement with a sharp needle at one end and a sealed connection at the other for attaching to a bag of blood, plasma, or saline. The whole set was sterile and contained in a plastic package, which he now held in his hands. In all his training for the job he now held, he had never been trained to administer intravenous fluids and had always hoped he would never have to do so—but here he was, with a sick man dependent on his ability to do it.

The names of so many hazardous cargoes went briefly through his mind—acrylonitrile, toluene-di-iso-cyanate, and many more. Lethal liquids on which the world's chemical and plastics industry depended and which were transported in bulk on ships like *Excelsior* and by people like Chris and his crew every day of the year, and yet where was the training to deal with their effects if they escaped or spilled?

In truth there was plenty of training, and Chris and his people had done it all—training for spillage, for fire, for decontamination, but the training was mainly in accident avoidance and containment, and the ship was well equipped with firefighting kit, with breathing apparatus, chemical protection suits, and the like. The ship's staff were frequently drilled in its use and occasionally had to deal with such incidents for real.

Chemical poisoning was therefore a very unlikely event but one which could conceivably happen. Again, the ship was technically well equipped—with manuals, checklists, and first-aid kits—even sterile packs for immediate intramuscular injection of atropine and adrenalin, and 'poppers' for the administration of amyl-nitrite under the nose of an unconscious victim to stimulate the heart.

What was not provided was thorough training in the use of the equipment for intravenous giving, either to combat chemical poisoning or, as in this case, medical assistance of another sort.

Funnily enough—although not at all funny—the only fatal accident aboard a chemical tanker in the fleet had its source in a cargo of tallow—boiled up animal bits! The ship had carried a large tank full of the stuff, and after discharging it, the crew had to clean the tank ready for the next cargo.

Due to heavy weather on sailing, access to the tank was not possible, so a few feet of water were pumped in and heated, to 'sweat' the tank and keep the remnants of tallow soft.

When the weather moderated, two Chinese crew members entered the tank to rig portable cleaning machines in place (high-pressure sprinklers on the end of big rubber hoses), and they did so—against all regulations and training—without testing the atmosphere. They climbed down into a layer of hydrogen sulphide and other noxious gases, with the inevitable result that they collapsed unconscious into the bottom of the tank.

The alarm was raised by the man watching them from the deck, and the emergency party mustered—to be told by the chief officer that it was 'only tallow' and not to bother with breathing apparatus! Three further men went down including the chief officer, and a total of five men lost their lives.

All these thoughts flicked quickly through Chris's mind as he checked the giving-set and looked at the bags of sterile saline which had come in from the deck. He mused on the fact that the company didn't train him effectively to administer intravenous fluids, so they wouldn't be held accountable. The words of his Marine Superintendent at the 'Hazardous Cargo Seminar' last year came to mind again—'Well, gentlemen, just pray you never have to do it, and if you do, remember that you could lay yourself open to a manslaughter charge if you cock it up—the company will be right behind you as long as you do it right!'

He realised that he was thinking himself into a negative state of mind—the last thing he needed—so he ran over what the doctors had told him: 'it's a piece of cake if you find a vein and control the shaking of your hands! Best place is in the arm, just below the elbow joint where it bends. If he's conscious, get him to hold something in his hand and squeeze rhythmically until you see the vein pop up. Then get him to clench his fist and slide the needle into the vein about a centimetre below the bulge, trying to enter at a shallow angle all the way in. You'll know when you're in because there'll be a bit of blood come back up the tube before you turn on the saline. If he's not conscious, hang his arm down for a bit, then try to squeeze the blood up from his hand and forearm to make the vein stand out. Get someone else to do that so you can be ready with the needle.'

'OK, guys, everybody out except you, Ted, and the chief steward. Chief, can you get a wire coat hanger and hang the saline up by the window like a hospital frame? Ted, you help me with the alcohol swabs and stuff, and be ready to help me with the procedure whatever happens. I just may feel a bit faint myself!'

At this, Dave, the pumpman—whom everyone seemed to have forgotten about for a moment—opened his eyes and said, 'Cap, I have every faith in you. Got no choice, have I?'

'OK, Dave, I think you know what we're going to do. Just put this needle into your arm and give you some saline to keep you going until the doctor gets here, OK? Feeling up to it?'

Dave smiled feebly and nodded. The first saline bag was rigged up by the window, and Chris opened the giving-set, attaching the valve to the bag and opening it slightly to fill the tube and flood liquid briefly out of the needle at the other end before the valve was closed again. He took a deep breath and nodded to the chief officer, who swabbed Dave's arm with alcohol and held it steady from the other side of the hospital bed.

Chris leaned over, gave Dave a pad of bandages to grip and flooded his own hands with alcohol before putting on a thin pair of latex gloves. While Dave gripped and released the pad, they all stared intently, looking for the vein. Nothing—not a sign of a bulge or a bluish line under the skin!

'OK, no problem' said Chris. 'Lower his arm. Dave, I want you to really grip hard. Now, Ted, in a couple of seconds grip his wrist tight and slide your grip up towards his elbow to move the blood up, OK?'

'That's it!—great—hold it tight but give me some room!' Chris slid the needle into the slightly raised vein which had appeared in Dave's arm, and immediately there was a puff of blood into the tube behind the needle. 'Got it!' shouted Chris. 'OK, Chief, turn on the valve—slowly now!'

As saline flowed down the tube into Dave's arm, two things happened—Dave let out a long, slow groan and passed out, and a swelling began to appear just in front of the needle entry point.

'Oh shit—fucking Christ!' said Chris. 'I think I've gone right through his bloody vein and out the other side. The saline is just filling up his skin! Right, Chief, turn it off. Ted, hold his arm steady.' Chris slowly withdrew the needle about a third of the way out, at which point another puff of blood appeared. He then angled it slightly up and reinserted it all the way in. 'Now try that again—valve open, Chief!'

As the valve was opened this time there was no increase in the swelling, which, if anything, was subsiding. Chris went around to the saline bag and watched the liquid dripping into the reservoir above the valve and the tube. It seemed to be flowing out as quickly as it was dripping in. 'I think we've done it guys! How is he?'

The chief steward checked Dave's pulse, which was weak and thready, but at least he had one! 'OK, I think—still out though, but he's breathing smoothly.'

'Right, Ted, quick swab and put a plaster over the needle entry point. Let's watch him and see how it goes. I'll get to the bridge and see if we can raise the *Arcturus* and the Coast Guard.'

Half an hour later Dave had recovered consciousness and had said he was tired—promptly falling asleep and snoring gently. He hadn't shown any blood for a while, but everyone knew that the saline was just a holding measure, and that more had to be done if he was to survive.

It was 0900 on the 9th onboard the *Excelsior*—1700 GMT—as the ship increased back up to full sea speed. Contact was regained with *Arcturus* and their courses slightly corrected to rendezvous. It looked as if they could meet up at approximately 1140 GMT, but that would be 0140 (10th) onboard *Excelsior* and fully dark. The decision was therefore made for *Arcturus* to reduce speed to enable a meeting at daybreak—0600 for *Excelsior*—1400 GMT or Zulu Time—as Chris had decided not to muck about with the ship's clocks until things had settled down a bit.

'Sparks, can you get me all the available updates on weather in our region for the next forty-eight hours?—general picture, wind and swell—the usual stuff but quick as you can please.' Chris's unease about the weather was growing, as the barometer was continuing to fall, and the swell was becoming more definite. He felt that he'd rather taken his eye off the ball in this respect, but he felt that he could forgive himself under the circumstances, and he certainly wasn't going to change the forecast by beating himself up about it.

The difficulties of launching a boat in a Pacific swell and, even more so, recovering it again safely, weren't to be underestimated even for a passenger ship which was used to using her boats to ferry passengers ashore. To get the doctor onboard the tanker wasn't going to be much fun either, as he'd have to scramble up a pilot ladder or a net while the fully laden ship rolled and pitched. Chris decided to call a meeting with the chief officer, the chief steward, the bosun, and the chief engineer to discuss and to plan as soon as Sparks had got the weather information together.

A quick call back to *Arcturus* reported to the doctors that the patient seemed stable although he was continuing to vomit blood every couple of hours and confirmed that she would use one of her boats—the 'crash boat,' which was a fast, manoeuvrable RIB generally used for man-overboard drills or realities.

'Thanks, Sparks—great job—and thanks everyone,' Chris said as he turned to the bridge team (which at that moment seemed to consist of nearly everyone onboard—on watch and off). He realised then that he'd never felt quite so lonely and yet quite so supported.

Not for the first time, Chris found himself fascinated by his reactions to involvement in things medical. He had actually enjoyed dealing with the saline drip, but at the same time he realised that he was out of his depth—out of his comfort zone.

True, as a child he thought he had wanted to be a doctor; he even started his secondary education with a medical career vaguely in mind, but he had then chosen a totally different path. Was he predestined to go to sea?—after all, his father had been at sea, and his brother had started out in that direction.

He didn't know; all he did know was that there had been times when he felt himself to be a complete misfit in his chosen career and times when he had come into contact with doctors and medical matters and felt irresistibly drawn towards them.

The irony was that he'd been, thus far, very successful at sea—winning prizes at college, passing his professional examinations and gaining promotion and subsequent command very young. Musing briefly now he recognised that perhaps the attributes required of either profession were in many ways similar—the ability to absorb large amounts of information, to focus, to make decisions, to provide leadership, to act independently, and to stand by the results of one's actions.

Another irony was that his elder brother, whom he was visiting on the training-ship when he changed his life direction, didn't want to be there—didn't want to go to sea. The poor chap wanted to be a farmer, but Dad had decided that he needed remedial treatment, so off he went!

What, Chris wondered, were the differentiators? What were the attributes or abilities which made one person more suited to be a doctor or a sea captain and the other person not? He recalled that in his career so far, the particular aspect of his character that had caused him most difficulty was his tendency to see both sides of any situation—to try to be too fair—to be perhaps too compassionate in a profession where compassion and human understanding were often suppressed by autocracy and the need for authoritative rule.

On the other hand, he could remember his mother telling him, at a fairly early age, that 'you'd never be any good as a doctor; you'd get too involved with the suffering of your patients—want to "get into bed" with them.'

Perhaps there was something in that. Did his feelings of being somewhat 'different' to most of his professional colleagues stem from character traits that were more suited to caring than commanding—that might even have been a cause of difficulty if he had pursued his original idea of a medical career?

Such introspection again! He shook himself out of it with the realisation that the here and now provided more than enough to think about and to do, so he'd better get on with it!

CHAPTER 6

READY, STEADY ...

'OK, guys, daybreak tomorrow we meet the *Arcturus*, and she'll lend us a doctor. They've apparently got two, but they won't lend us the senior one as she's an attractive woman!'—a brief chuckle all 'round. 'How's the patient, Chief?'

The chief steward—never a very articulate man except when he was complaining about somebody or something—said, 'Getting weaker, I reckon—still conscious as long as he's lying flat, but still losing blood.'

'Is the blood fresh or old?'

'Christ's sake, I don't know. It's just blood, isn't it?' said the chief steward, visibly turning paler.

'I mean does it look fresh as if he's still bleeding somewhere, or old and dark, like coffee grounds?'

'Oh—fresh, I reckon—probably why he's weaker. I didn't know aspirins could do this damage!'

'Chief, that's not the problem now, and you were doing your best,' Chris said rather more charitably than he felt.

'Don't give him anything at all by mouth. The saline will stop him dehydrating, and let me know if anything changes at all—colour, pulse, anything, OK? You can leave us to it now, and thanks.'

Turning to the others, Chris laid out the meteorological faxes on the chart table and explained: 'We've got a good picture of the sea and swell conditions for tomorrow, and a comprehensive general weather picture. It doesn't look good—not a hurricane exactly, but the mother of a storm brewing—a sort of semi-tropical revolving storm.'

The tropical revolving storm, or TRS, was something Chris remembered first learning about in the training ship—in fact, it had been a mark of status and seniority to swagger about the decks talking about it while the younger cadets could only listen in awe at the wisdom and knowledge of their 16-year-old seniors.

The natural circulation of air around an area of low pressure down near the equator, the process of sucking in more warm, moist air to provide energy and the gradual speeding up of that circulation, resulting in the formation of an almost perfect machine for redistributing that energy in the form of wind and rain—this is the TRS. Hundreds of miles across, it is known by different names in different parts of the world—cyclone in the Indian Ocean and the Bay of Bengal, hurricane in the Atlantic, Caribbean, and south Pacific, typhoon in the northern Pacific and the China Sea—even as a 'Willie-Willie' in old Australian sea-lore. It is to be treated with the utmost respect and, at best, avoided altogether.

'So, what do we reckon? It'll be brewing up nicely by this time tomorrow—just our bloody luck—or Dave's.'

'What side of the storm are we on, Chris?' The use of his first name on the bridge by the chief officer was comforting on this occasion, suggesting that this was a meeting of professional colleagues, working together, rather than a group of men expecting their captain to know all the answers and solve all the problems while they just did as they were told.

'That's the other bit of bad news, Ted. We're going to be slap in the dangerous semicircle. If we use the time we've got in hand before morning to rendezvous somewhere else, all we can do is put ourselves smack in the path of it or steer out of it a bit hoping it doesn't change direction itself. It's due to turn pretty soon, I reckon, looking at its track!'

They were alluding to the fact that, as the storm rotates and moves along its path, a ship can find herself either on that side of it where she will be, literally, thrown out of its path, or drawn into it. If she's likely to be drawn into its path, then she's in the 'dangerous semicircle' and—in theory at least—should do her best to get out of it. Such storms tend to recurve as they mature—turn their path through up to ninety degrees, thus occasionally thwarting any attempts to avoid them.

'Well,' said Chris, 'Dave needs help, and our best bet is to get that doctor onboard with his kit. At least then he's got a good chance. We may need to transfer Dave and the doc onto the *Arcturus*, but that may be pushing our luck by the look of the weather. At least the doc is fit to travel, and the passenger ship seems to have the sort of boat to make it fairly safe.'

'So, we need to be prepared to heave-to and receive the doc,' said the chief officer. 'We can rig a long line along the lee side of the ship—forward to aft just above the water, and a stores net over the side by the manifold—could even spread some fish oil to flatten things down a bit.' A couple of good hands on the deck to lower a lifeline, and we'll have him onboard in a tick!'

'Sounds good Ted. Remember we need to get all his kit onboard too, but if his people have that all boxed up and a line attached, they can give us the line, and we can drag it onboard while we grab the doc.'

The bosun suggested an alternative idea. 'Can't we float a life raft down to the *Arcturus* on a long line, then heave him back to us in the raft? I've done that before.'

'Well, thanks bo's; it would mean him boarding the raft on the windward side of *Arcturus*. I guess they could float a raft down to us, but then the doc would have to board us on our windward side. No, I think I feel happier with the crash boat coming to our leeward side, and I'm sure the doc will feel the same too. We'll keep your idea as a backup in case they decide they can't launch. Get the six-man raft from forward and have it by the manifold with a long warp of good rope, just in case.

OK. Ted, what about the fish oil?'

'Well, oil on troubled waters, you know. I've got loads of old samples in the locker, and a few litres will do—spread it from forward of the manifold, slowly, before the boat comes alongside. They won't like the smell, but it'll wash off with hot water, and it may make a big difference even if we make a good lee.'

'OK, then, let's do that. Chief, any problems?' Chris turned to the chief engineer.

'No, just give us two hours' notice to slow her down and cool off, then we'll go onto light diesel in case we need to manoeuvre; two steering motors on, and we'll be ready for anything.'

'Fine, Bob, thanks. And medical-wise let's have first aid kit and blankets up on deck, and some hot coffee ready for our visitor—oh, and a bottle of good malt in a bag to send back to the *Arcturus*'s captain, eh?' Ted will you tell the chief steward?'

———〰———

Onboard *Arcturus*, Jonathan was excited and apprehensive. 'At last!' he thought. 'At last some real sea action and some real doctoring again!' The truth was that having made the decision to take a year or two out of mainstream medicine and go off to sea, he'd been bored stiff once the initial novelty had worn off—not feeling that he was learning anything about the sea of his father's dreams or doing anything medically useful.

Brenda Hollingsworth, the senior surgeon, had given him the details of the plan developed by the captains of the two ships, and they had just finished discussing the medical situation. 'You'll be transferred in the crash boat at dawn tomorrow. The weather may be really bad, so it'll be hairy, but apparently quite safe! The other ship will spread oil on the water and provide shelter, while our crew deliver you alongside. The tanker will throw you a lifeline which you'll attach to your harness, then you'll need to scramble up their boarding net onto the deck. The boat's crew will deliver your kit onboard for you. Oh, and if we can't get you off again, you'll have to stay with them to Honolulu! By the sound of it, your patient will be too sick to move over here, even if the weather allowed it, so take some clean underwear with you and a few seasick tablets!'

'God, Brenda! Are you really going to send me off on this … this jaunt?'

'It's not a jaunt, Jonathan, and yes, I think you need it. You've been swanning around here complaining that you're bored, boring *us* with stories of your father and how you could have been a senior deck officer by now, so it'll do you good to see how the other half live! And …' she said with a smile, 'you know that you're good in an emergency and a good doctor—you'd be wasted on the bridge!'

Now he was gathering his thoughts and his equipment in the sophisticated and under-used surroundings of the *Arcturus*'s hospital dispensary. As agreed with Brenda, he'd need plenty of refrigerated saline—really cold. He'd need to improvise for introducing cold saline into the patient's stomach and for getting it out again, but he had clear ideas on that and had gathered various lengths of rubber tubing, connectors and nozzles.

While the diagnosis was reasonably clear-cut, they couldn't be certain, so he had to be prepared for alternatives. What did that mean? If there was a rupture below the stomach, there wasn't much he could do on his own except to provide more blood and keep the guy alive until they made port.

The captain had broadcast to the ship a little earlier, asking passengers and crew if there were any among them who were regular blood donors with their cards onboard, with type 'O' blood, and who would be willing to make a quick donation. So far two people had come forward and were being bled right then, so that side of things looked reasonable.

'Defibrillator, portable heart monitor, throat anaesthetic, gag, antibiotics—better take some Valium—oh, and some

Stugeron for me!' He worked as he thought, gathering stuff together ready for a final meeting with his boss.

—— ⁓⁓ ——

'Ted, we'd better double up the watch from 0400, and could you make sure we've got the very best of our seamen on deck for the transfer?' Chris was having a quiet discussion with the chief officer.

'I've fixed the watches, boss, and we've got Roddy and Knocky on daywork this month. Murdo will be about too. We'll have all hands available anyway, but the bosun will make sure those three are there to receive the lines and the gear et cetera. They're dry at the moment, too!'

'Good Ted, thanks.' All Hebrideans—Roddy and Knocky were from Stornoway on Lewis,—had joined together and were inseparable, while Murdo was from Harris. They spoke their own quiet Gaelic dialect together most of the time. All ex-fishermen, they were natural seamen and totally reliable if they stayed off the whisky.

'OK, then, we all know what needs to be done. Let's get everyone together again on the bridge before dinner tonight, just to finalise things. And thanks again to everybody. Keep everyone else in the picture and pray that the weather holds off. Feel the swell building?' Ted nodded and they separated to get on with their preparations.

—— ⁓⁓ ——

Lunchtime—nobody was particularly hungry, but Chris thought he'd better put on a show of being unworried. In reality he was worried—worried for Dave, and for the boat's crew and the doctor—couldn't stop the continuous barrage of 'what ifs' and the constant urge to go and stare at the weather maps, stay on the bridge, as if he could will the weather to moderate and the time to pass more swiftly.

He went to the serving hatch in the saloon and waited while the steward finished bantering with a few of the men at the opposite hatch. When he came over, he said, 'Sorry, Captain—bloody Chookters!—don't know when to stop talking, but at least I'm beginning to understand their accents!' This was a bit rich coming from Stevie, as he was so Liverpudlian that he was often virtually unintelligible to southern ears.

'Oh, yes, what are they on about, Stevie?'

'Oh, you know, Cap—how they're going to save the day tomorrow, only real seamen onboard—bosun's chosen few. And the likelihood—or lack of it—of double overtime and a free drink afterwards! Oh, and Pete's started a book on whether we get the doc onboard without him gettin' his feet wet and whether the pumpman croaks beforehand!'

Chris was cheered to know that these men were behaving in the normal fashion of the merchant seaman—humorously cynical, thinking of the money but willing and able to do a dangerous job well and get little official thanks for it. Also, that it probably hadn't occurred to them that he would be worried or that he wouldn't be able to do his job.

He suddenly remembered his Dad, telling him as a youngster about his own experience: 'I went on the bridge to take the watch for the first time on my own—legs shaking, knees knocking, and my heart in my mouth. Everyone was closed-up, just doing their routine jobs effectively, and nobody thought to doubt me—so I just got on with it. After that first time it got a little easier.'

'Chief steward's shitting bricks though!—stupid bastard!—and all he seems to care about is his bloody shoes!' Chris knew that the chief steward wasn't held in very high esteem by his team. Everyone knew that he was on the make—'taking the food out of our mouths he is!' was their unspoken comment. The nearest Chris had come to catching him out was over the bacon.

Last port in the US Gulf—the last place you'd want to buy stores due to the expense—he phoned one morning to say, 'That bacon I thought we had turns out to be gammon steaks! I'll need to buy a case before we sail.' Fait-accompli, really—Chris couldn't envisage taking the ship right across the Pacific without the boys being able to have their bacon sarnies of a morning. So, he'd said OK—not feeling quite sure about it though. Later on, he'd wandered down to the chief's office and said, 'D'you get the bacon OK, Chief?'

'Yes, boss. Invoice is here, look.'

'OK, let's go and have a look at it. I don't want the boys to be disappointed with American bacon without me knowing what it's like!'

'You don't need to worry about that. It's just like our other stuff, and I've unpacked it and put it in the cool room with what little we had left.'

'I'd still like to see it,' said Chris, so they went down to the fridge flat, the chief mumbling about 'fucking waste of time—nothing better to do' and other things under his breath.

There was the bacon—all similar—nothing to show that it was American, or new, or different.

'OK, Chief, I think I know what you're up to. How much did the chandler give you in the brown envelope?'

'What the fuck d'you mean, Captain? You just say that one more time, and I'll have the union onto you like a ton of bricks. I'll bloody sue you too—gold braid or no gold braid!'

'No, Chief, no you won't. I'm onto your game, and you won't be sailing with us again. I can't prove it this time but be warned!' With that, he'd walked away, feeling angry and impotent, knowing that the catering manager in London was just as bad and that there'd be no backing from that quarter. Determined though that the chief steward wasn't going to do anything to undermine the morale onboard. Another thing Chris's dad had said—God knows when!—Keep the food good but give the men something else to grumble about, and they'll be happy—and if you're lucky they'll be on your side.'

Having had a small plate of fish and chips, Chris checked on the pumpman—pale, saline dripping into his arm, sleeping restlessly while being watched over by the junior steward.

He then went to his office, shuffled a few papers but couldn't settle and decided to lie down and read for a bit. On his daybed he picked up a book which had not ceased to intrigue him from the moment he started reading it—*The Time Traveller's Wife*, by Audrey Niffenegger, an implausible but beautiful tale about a man who time-travelled back and forth, meeting the girl he was to marry when she was very young and, at various times, seeing or meeting himself—as a child, as a young adult, and even as an old man.

He couldn't get back into it just then, but he started to think about it, staring at the fireproof plastic panels above his head and shifting gently to the roll of the ship on the ever-increasing swell.

'What if I could travel back in time and meet myself as a youngster? What would I say to me? Would I—could I—say anything to try and alter my future?

'No, the future can't be changed; it will happen because it *does* happen, because it is configured and informed by the past and by the present, and anybody coming from the future knows what *did* happen—what *will* happen when that future point is reached.

'So, what would be the point? What benefit might it bring? God, how many times have I wished I'd had someone to counsel me—just to help me understand. How many times have I thought "I wish I could have been kinder to myself as a kid—wish I could have coached me—nurtured me—perhaps even loved me!"'

With a sudden rush of insight and clarity he realised—perhaps for the first time ever—that he'd actually always been pretty hard on himself—had always given himself impossible standards to live up to—never being good enough to be happy with himself or his performance. Even now with whatever the morning would bring, he knew that he would be his own worst critic and that whatever his crew or anyone else thought about how he conducted himself, he'd probably be dissatisfied with himself and conduct all sorts of internal post-mortems afterwards—to the point that he'd convince himself that he was a complete failure, whatever the outcome.

His biggest battle would be to control these thoughts and the emotions that they would engender. But no, he was at least good at that—the negative introspection would come later. When he was 'on stage' (as he always felt on such occasions—out of his own body, observing himself as if he were someone else) he would be calm, efficient, and professional.

Chris sighed. 'Maybe there is something for me in this book,' he thought. 'Maybe I *can* counsel myself from the outside, as it were.'

'Chris, you've thought it through, you've covered all the bases. You've got a good team around you who are capable and willing to do a good job. The ship is fine—she's on your side too because she's well looked after. You're highly trained and experienced, highly intuitive with the ship and the weather. What more can you do?'

Chris fell asleep, the book unread on his chest. When he awoke an hour later, it was to the realisation that the swell had continued to develop and, on checking the barograph in his cabin, that the barometric pressure was falling more quickly. The word *hurricane* again came into his mind, and he went up to the bridge to read the pilot books—berating himself that he hadn't done so earlier.

CHAPTER 7

HURRICANE!

'Oh, Captain, I was about to give you a shout,' said the second mate as Chris arrived on the bridge. 'We've just got this in—weather warning!'

'Shit, are they declaring it a hurricane then?'—rhetorical question as the answer had been forming itself in Chris's subconscious for hours.

'Yup—severe storm, becoming a hurricane in the next twelve hours. I'm just plotting it on the chart in relation to our rendezvous. Looking at the text I think we'll just be on the edge, but you never know what these things are going to do.'

OK, sec—you plot it up, with forward movements of us and the storm for the next few days. I'll have a look at the *Pilot Book*.

Chris walked over to the bookcase on the aft bulkhead—the pilot books published by the British Admiralty were arranged there in order—detailed navigational and other information for virtually every sea and coast in the world.

He pulled out number 62—*Pacific Islands Pilot Volume 3*— and turned to the meteorological information near the front.

There he found a history of the tropical storms and hurricanes which had passed close to the Hawaiian Islands over the past one hundred or so years. He was alarmed to read that they were more frequent than he had imagined— most of the stuff he'd read or seen about Hawaii stressed its wonderful and settled climate! One in the early 1950s had been particularly bad, virtually destroying the season's sugar cane crop and causing great loss of life—nothing too bad since, though.

He looked at the diagram showing typical hurricane tracks, but this wasn't of much help as they seemed to come into the islands from every direction—although the predominant overall track was from south-east to north-west initially, altering course towards the north-east at some stage.

'OK, Cap,' said the second mate, 'it's on the chart.' Chris looked across to see the ship's current position, the proposed rendezvous point, and the track they'd probably need to make for Honolulu thereafter, drawn lightly in 2b pencil on the paper chart.

The ocean chart was too small a scale for this, so the second mate had added a blank piece of old chart-paper to the side of the Hawaiian Islands chart to extend it to the north and east. This way they were able to plot more accurately, and the second mate (the official navigator and responsible for upkeep of the charts) was happy to have used a red colour-pencil to plot the storm centre with concentric rings around it. This too was plotted forward to show its forecast probable movement.

'Hurricane Iniki then—well, we seem to be fairly well away from the centre, don't we—the trade-wind is only force five and from the east north-east, but look at that swell.' They turned to the windows and looked for a few moments at the long ocean swell coming onto their port bow. 'That's risen considerably. It's opposing the direction of the normal ocean swell from the trade winds, which fits with the chart but doesn't help us. Just don't want two swells together, do we? Remember?'

The second mate and Chris had sailed together before, when Chris had been a young chief officer. They had shared the experience of being in a cargo ship off the coast of South Africa when she had been hit by a 'double swell wave'—the combination of two swells, at right angles to each other, whose troughs had coincided and almost swallowed the ship. Derricks all over the place, wires over the side, the forward hatch stove in, and even the bridge windows smashed—fifty feet above the sea surface.

'Yes, what an experience that was, but given her present track we should be OK for the rendezvous. What happens after that depends on whether she recurves! They're forecasting a probable turn once she's past the islands, and that could place us smack in her path!'

'That's the dilemma all right, Tim, but if we're going to get Dave some help it's a risk we'll have to take. Looking on the bright side, she may not recurve, and if she does, she may be well to the west of us, and … That's a lot of maybes and maybe-nots! Let's hope for the best and prepare for the worst, eh?'

Chris left the bridge to confer with the chief engineer and to check on Dave. He took the pilot book with him, along with the rather tattered and salt-stained bridge copy of *Meteorology for Mariners* so that he could refresh himself on the habits of tropical storms and how to avoid them.

CHAPTER 8

RENDEZVOUS

C hris had met with his team on the bridge at 6 p.m. Plans had been reviewed, and all was confirmed to be as ready as it could be. Dave was showing signs of being weaker—still losing a significant amount of blood occasionally and spending more time in a semiconscious state—not asleep but not awake either. Chris was more worried than he let on.

He briefed everyone on the weather situation, showing them the plot and the various facsimile maps, explaining what they meant. 'By this time in the morning, the wind should still be moderate—six to seven—but the swell will be really significant, and probably shorter, almost at right angles to the wind.' That meant that if he made a lee—a sheltered side for the boat to come alongside—the swell would be running along the side of the ship. This could work in their favour, as it meant that the heavily laden tanker should not be rolling too much, just pitching. Chris intended to heave-to with the wind on his port side and the swell coming from ahead. In this way he could move gently ahead to maintain steerageway, and the boat could come in around *Excelsior*'s stern onto her starboard side to deposit the doctor and his kit onboard.

'Remember to keep everyone and everything up on the flying bridge in the shelters, until I give you the word. We should raise *Arcturus* on VHF at about 0400, so any changes to the plan after I've spoken to her, I'll let you know straight away. Have everyone booted and spurred for then, please. I know they're cumbersome, but anyone going on deck must wear harnesses and life jackets and, of course, safety helmets, OK?' Various nods of assent and understanding, and the team dispersed to eat and to work or relax in their various ways.

Saturday, 11 September. Three thirty in the morning, or 11.30 a.m. GMT. Chris wasn't sure if he'd slept or not. Certainly not much or very soundly. He got up and had a quick, cold shower, towelled himself off, and put on a clean uniform shirt and shorts. He could already feel the engine speed changing as they began to reduce revolutions, so the watch officer had given the required two hours' notice to manoeuvre as planned.

On the bridge he was greeted by the second officer who quickly made him some coffee and assured him that they hadn't heard anything from *Arcturus* on VHF. 'Tried to raise them at 0300 but no joy. I'll give them another call.'

The chief officer joined them on the bridge to take over the watch. He hadn't slept much either, so he'd got up a bit early. 'Tell you what, Ted,' said Chris, 'I'll take over the watch, then you can check everything's ready to go. Get the third mate out to be with you. Sec, I'd like you to stay with me on the bridge—you can have a lie-in later!' From the shadows by the door, the third officer said, 'No need to call me! I couldn't sleep either!'

The second officer went over to the VHF set on the main console and picked up the handset. Checking that it was on channel 16 and on the speaker, he squeezed the transmit button: '*Arcturus, Arcturus*, this is British Chemical Tanker *Excelsior* calling *Arcturus*. Over.'

A crackle of static, indicating that someone was transmitting nearby but just out of range. A cup of coffee and ten minutes later, Chris had taken over the watch and tried again with the VHF radio. This time *Arcturus* was clearly heard responding—still not clear enough for a conversation, but at least contact was made. Step one.

Within thirty minutes clear contact had been made with *Arcturus*, a working radio channel agreed in order to keep the calling channel clear and positions exchanged. Both ships had made a minor alteration of course and were looking out for each other on radar. The two captains confirmed their plans:

'*Excelsior*, this is *Arcturus*. G'morning, Chris. Colin here. Over.'

'*Arcturus*, this is *Excelsior*. Good morning, Colin, good to hear you. Are you still happy with the plan? Over.'

'*Excelsior, Arcturus*. Roger that, Chris. Our Baby Doc is all ready to go. We'll launch from a good lee with a crew of four including the doc. The seamen are all tried and tested, and our boat is the latest RIB—bit like a motorbike really but with a jet impeller so there's no danger from trailing ropes. Over.'

'Sounds good. We'll make a lee on our starboard side, head to swell. We're getting wind force six to seven, so we may spread a bit of fish oil to quieten things down if necessary. That OK with you? Over.'

'OK, Chris. We could both turn full-circle before the transfer, to make a patch of quieter water, but with a lot of elderly passengers and God knows how much crockery onboard, I don't want to do that. You may be able to though—might save covering our boat with fish oil! Over.'

'Good idea, Colin. I can warn everyone and take a round-turn before your boat comes alongside. We'll need to time it just right if it's going to work though. Over.'

'Roger that, Chris. I suggest we make the transfer say, three cables apart, at two knots, you astern of me, and that we have all communications on this channel, 12, so we each know what's going on with the other. Over.'

'OK, Colin. Formal communications from now on. Oh, we have you on radar now—at least we have a ship distant twenty-two miles bearing 236 true. Over.'

'*Excelsior* bridge, *Arcturus* bridge. Yes, we have you too— reducing speed now to rendezvous in fifty minutes. Over.'

'*Arcturus* bridge, *Excelsior* bridge. Listening on this channel. Out.'

Step two.

Everything was ready. The sun was just rising as the two ships came in sight of one another. *Arcturus* looked quite majestic—huge and white, hardly rolling in the long five-metre-high swell as her stabilisers smoothed her passage.

Shortly she would have to bring them in, but she would turn into the swell before then. *Excelsior*, on the other hand, was pitching and rolling heavily to the swell coming in on her port bow. With her deck being only eight feet above the waterline, it was often awash, and the deck party were staying safely up on the 'flying bridge' with their various pieces of equipment at the ready. This long catwalk extended from the front of her accommodation block to the forecastle, with several 'bus shelters' spaced out along its length for refuge.

At one mile distance, *Arcturus* turned slowly to starboard to face the swell coming from the south, while *Excelsior* passed behind her.

Three long minutes later: '*Excelsior* bridge, *Arcturus* bridge. Preparing to launch. When are you making your turn? Over.'

'*Arcturus* bridge, *Excelsior* bridge. We'll turn on your launch. Out! *Excelsior* deck, you all ready, Ted? Over.'

'*Excelsior bridge*, deck. All ready, Captain. Out.'

'*Excelsior*, *Arcturus* bridge. Launching now! Crash boat, away you go and good luck. Over!'

'*Arcturus*, *Excelsior* bridge. Turning now. Over.'

Chris had *Excelsior*'s helm put hard over to starboard. The engines had been on 'standby' for twenty minutes, and he had reduced to 'slow ahead' and then 'dead slow'. Now he gave the order for 'full ahead' to kick the ship into a fast turn. She swung, slowly at first and then faster and faster, putting *Arcturus* right ahead about three hundred yards distant, but continuing to turn through another full, tight circle before steadying up with the huge passenger ship right ahead again, about six hundred yards away. 'Dead slow ahead', and she slowed quickly, rising to the big, steady swell.

While they were turning, the second officer had been relaying the distance to *Arcturus* as shown on the radar. He had seen the echo of the crash boat's radar-reflector detach itself from the passenger ship and begin its journey. 'Textbook, Captain!' he shouted—'three cables!' He walked to the bridge windows and grabbed his binoculars, lining up with his captain's direction until he saw the crash boat surfing towards them down the front of the swell.

'Making heavy weather of it on top of the swells!' said Chris to no one in particular. 'Oh Christ! Sec, call Ted and tell him to spread some of that fish oil—bugger the smell!'

As the little crash boat approached the bow of *Excelsior*, they could see two people sitting astride the centre pillion and two others crouched in the hull, well down and well drenched. They assumed rightly that everyone was attached with a lifeline and that there was an emergency engine cut-off attached to the coxswain of the boat. Suddenly a slick of glass bloomed from *Excelsior*'s starboard bow where one of the deck team had slowly emptied a few sample bottles of fish oil into the scupperway, and it had run overboard. The oil spread quickly on the water alongside the ship—until now hugely agitated by the wind sucking in around bow and stern—and it suddenly flattened.

Now their manoeuvres were paying off. The tight turn had created a circle of propeller-wash which was effectively blocking the worst of the swell waves from breaking. The oil flattened the wind-waves alongside the ship just as the crash boat shot past and carried out a high-speed turn towards them. Four white faces were fixed on *Excelsior*'s deck amidships while on that deck Roddy and Knocky Mcleod, secured with safety ropes and lifejackets, stood poised to throw heaving lines to the boat when required.

The crash boat came alongside, and Ted, the chief officer, on the deck by this time, heard the coxswain say to his pillion rider—'when I say jump, you fucking *jump*. OK? G'luck, mate!'

The seamen in the boat quickly looped their attached lines around the 'boat-rope'—a thick rope draped along *Excelsior*'s side. Rising and falling as they were to the swell, the boat-rope was slack enough for the boat to ride reasonably alongside. Baby Doc swung his leg over the pillion and got ready to jump for the cargo net.

'Not yet!' cried Roddy. Attach this line to yersel',' and he threw his heaving line down. The doctor quickly tied it to the 'D-ring' on his combined harness and inflatable jacket and got ready to jump.

'Wait for it, wait for it—*now jump!*' said the coxswain, and Baby Doc leapt for the cargo net shouting 'Yeehah' as he went. He'd jumped at the top of the swell, so he was only a couple of feet below the deck, and a combination of his scrabbling and Roddy pulling soon got him on deck as the boat fell away like an express lift.

Meanwhile, Knocky had passed his line down to the other seaman, who had attached the first of the medical kit. It was onboard in a moment, and Roddy's line now went down for the remainder.

In seconds it was all done. The coxswain screamed, 'Leggo!' and the jet-drive roared as the boat pulled away. 'Bloody Chookters!' he yelled. 'Look at all this stinking crap on my boat!'

'Welcome onboard *Excelsior*,' said Ted to the white-faced doctor. 'You OK? You look a bit pale!'

'Yeah, fine' said the doc. 'Does she always move like this?'

Step three.

On the '*Excelsior*'s' bridge, Chris had been a mere spectator—alertly poised to do whatever was necessary, but his team had done exactly what was required, and exactly to plan. Now the focus of everyone's attention had to be on the crash boat as she buffeted against wind and swell to get back to her mothership.

There had been constant radio traffic between the two craft during the transfer, so Chris had not added to it—just listened. '*Arcturus* mobile to Mother. Transfer completed, returning to ship. Over.'

'Mother here, mobile. Well done. I can't turn off the swell without injuring passengers, but we'll keep a good lee. I'll leave you in peace. Out.'

Above the promenade deck of *Arcturus*, poised on the davit-platform for the crash boat, the chief officer and his team were preparing to recover their boat and its crew. This was probably the most dangerous part of the whole mission as that small boat had to manoeuvre under her lifting-crane, hook on, and be lifted clear of the water all the while rising and falling to the now steepening swell. The people in the boat were at risk from the crane-hook, from loose loops of wire, and from the risk of crushed fingers as they hooked on and tried to remain so.

Their training was thorough, but it had all been done in relatively calm conditions. Now, however, they went through the drill in their minds until the boat appeared beneath them.

'Right, bo'sun—painter!' shouted the chief officer, and a long rope streaked down from the promenade deck to be caught by the bow man in the boat and deftly attached with a toggle. This 'painter' came from a long way forward in the ship, so it gave a long, stretchy line at a low angle and, as the boat reduced her speed the ship towed her gently, and she stayed reasonably alongside. Some fish oil washing off the smaller craft perhaps helped too, in smoothing the water—although the coxswain would never admit this.

'Lower the falls!'—and the crane hook, dangling a soft rope, descended to the boat. The coxswain grabbed the rope and guided the hook in, allowing a good length of wire to flake down between the boat and the ship's side. Once he judged that there was enough scope in the wire to allow for the swell, the coxswain indicated the crane operator to stop and attached the boat's bridle to the crane hook.

The bow and stern men in the boat had ensured that the four-part 'bridle' was ready. One wire from each corner of the wider parts of the boat led to a central ring, so that the boat could be raised stably and horizontally.

As the boat fell on the receding swell the crane wire became almost taut. As she started to rise again the coxswain, holding the hook-rope and keeping his fingers well clear of the hook, screamed 'heave away!' The wire gathered in, became taut, and the boat rose quickly just ahead of the rising swell. Her crew, sitting well down and clear of the bridle, hung on for dear life until the hook reached the top of its travel and willing hands grabbed the side of the boat to secure it inboard.

Step four.

'*Arcturus*, this is *Excelsior*. Over.'

'*Excelsior, Arcturus*. Hello, Chris. Well done.' Over.'

'Colin, I don't know how to thank you—and your people, especially your boat's crew. Please just accept the grateful thanks of all here for the moment. Over.'

'Thank you, Chris, but it's just the end of the beginning isn't it? How's your man? Over.'

'Not sure. Your doctor is having a look at him now. By the look of the forecast, we're not going to be doing any further transfers of patient *or* doctor, are we? Over.'

'Agree with you there. I propose that we stay with you until the doctor has assessed your patient, then we make further plans. If we both proceed towards Honolulu at your best speed, we can't go too far wrong, can we? Over.'

'Roger that. D'you have any later updates on the storm? Over.'

'Probably the same as you—latest we've got is that she's classified as a hurricane, named Iniki and likely to recurve soon. Over.'

'Yep, same here, Colin. Will you go into Honolulu if she's around there? Over.'

'Well, that's the question isn't it? If she turns, I'll probably try to get around behind her, even if it means delaying our arrival further. I don't know what the passengers will think of that. At the moment they're in two camps—those that are part of the adventure and want to know how your man is minute by minute and those who are already calling their lawyers! Over.'

'I know we need to keep our sick man as first priority, but I'd rather be outside with clear sea-room in a big blow! Anyway, we'll see what she does, and meanwhile we can make twelve knots—direct course for Diamond Point and Honolulu. I'll give you a call as soon as your doc has told me what he thinks. And thanks again, Colin. Over and out.'

'*Excelsior, Arcturus*. No problem, Chris. Listening on 12 and 16. Out.'

CHAPTER 9

MEDICAL ASSESSMENT

C hris was in his cabin thirty minutes later when Jonathan, the 'baby doc,' knocked on his office door. 'Come in!' said Chris, and they met for the first time—two men in their mid-thirties, both secure in their different professions and both willing to be respectful of the other's differing experience and knowledge.

'Well, hello, Captain. I thought it best to get down to see your man as soon as I could, but thanks for the reception party! That was a rush, I can tell you!'

'I bet it was, and welcome onboard! Thank you for coming. I can't tell you how personally grateful I am. What d'you think of the patient?'

'Much as you described really—gastric tear—probably the duodenum, but you seem to have done all the right things. I don't like the look of his blood pressure; he must have lost a lot of blood, so I've put him straight onto a transfusion of the whole stuff. The saline has kept him going, but we must stop the bleeding as soon as he's strong enough.'

'How will you do that? Oh, sorry—would you like a coffee or something—breakfast perhaps?'

Jonathan indicated that he probably wasn't ready for solid food again yet. 'I'm afraid I've been spoiled with stabilisers in my sea-going career, but I'm on the tablets so I'll be OK! What I'd like to do is carry out a "gastric lavage"—literally wash him out with ice-cold saline to seal the tear and hopefully stop the bleeding. I don't think anything has perforated through the duodenum. A ruptured vein should respond quite quickly, but we'll have to be really careful not to puncture through!'

'OK, then,' said Chris. 'I imagine you're onboard for the duration, so I'll let *Arcturus* know that she can get on her way?'

Chris thought that he detected a look of slight relief on the face of the young doctor, as he said, 'Yes, I'm here until Honolulu. I wouldn't want to try and transfer him to Mother in his state. Mind you, by the time we get him into hospital *Arcturus* may well have sailed for Auckland, and I'll be on the beach! They'll probably get someone else out and fly me home.' A wry grin and again that slight look of relief?

'Well, we're pleased to have you! Call me Chris, by the way, but do I detect a slight touch of something else in your reaction to being here?'

'Ah, Chris—call me Jonathan—life is complicated isn't it? And maybe we go out to complicate it further! Suffice to say that life at sea on a floating geriatric ward hasn't turned out to be quite what I'd expected!'

'Mm, well maybe we could talk about all that sometime! OK, I'll see you later. I'll talk to *Arcturus* so she can get on her way.

Having spoken again to the captain of *Arcturus* and agreed that she should proceed at her own best speed, Chris was asked to get Jonathan to the radio to brief his senior doctor.

Jonathan duly arrived back on the bridge and gave his boss a clear picture of his diagnosis and his plans, after which she asked a question which took him aback. 'What's all this with Jennifer then, Jon? She's in a hell of a state and as much use to me as a rag doll!—says she wants to talk to you, OK?'

'Oh God, Bren. OK, put her on.'

There was a small delay while Jennifer was instructed in the use of the handset, and there she was, slightly out of breath.

'Well, I knew you wanted to get away from me, but this is a bit much! I'm sure you're doing a good job, but when will you be back here?'

Hi, Jen, good to hear you. I don't know—depends on the patient, the weather, and if we'll be able to link up—the ships I mean. Anyway, I didn't want to get away from you— just needed some space and a sense of doing something useful.'

'Are we going anywhere together, Jon—emotionally I mean?—or am I just a distraction for the voyage? I know what it feels like!'

'Jen, I honestly don't know. For my part, it started off as fun, then became more serious—I'm guessing for you in particular—but it's not been real life has it? Maybe this time apart will give us—me—some clarity.'

'This time apart? We may not see each other again this voyage—or perhaps any other!'

Jonathan realised that she was getting more wound up and that on a VHF radio link a lot of people could be eavesdropping! He really did care about her, but at this minute he just wanted to end the call.

'Jen, I promise I'll stay in touch, and I promise we'll talk properly when we can sit down together, OK? Now I must go and see my patient. Sending you my love. Over and out!'

CHAPTER 10

ANXIOUS TIMES

Experience had taught Chris to get his head down when he could, so now, with the doctor onboard and the ship riding well to the increasing swell, he went to his bunk. He calmed himself by reliving the past few hours and recognising that, so far, everyone had done a good job and that now, everyone knew what they had to do. The doc was able to get whole blood into his patient and to prepare for the gastric lavage. Although it sounded fairly straightforward, Chris couldn't imagine how that was going to be performed, but that wasn't really his concern. He slept solidly for five hours, surprisingly un-troubled by self-doubt.

He was woken by the coincidence of something beyond his consciousness and a phone call from the bridge. The feeling that something was changing, alerting him to possible danger, and the duty officer telling him that the sea-state was getting more confused. What was in fact happening was that the natural wind-driven swell from the north-east trades, which had been lifting their stern fairly comfortably, was now being confronted by another pattern, from ahead, generated by the approaching hurricane. Although both swell patterns were long and low, they opposed each other and occasionally cancelled each other out, but equally occasionally compounded together to form one big swell. It was this that gave the ship an increasing feeling of being on a roller-coaster. Much more, and she would start 'pounding'—her bow coming clear of the water and her fairly flat tanker's bottom slamming back down onto the surface, shaking the whole ship, jarring teeth, and causing the whole accommodation block to oscillate back and forth 'like a fiddler's elbow' as someone had once described it. Chris went to the bridge where he could see the sea surface and align his senses to those of his ship.

Going to sea was, by its very nature, a dangerous profession compared to most, but most seafarers were trained for it. Chemical tankers had their own added risks, but again, people were specifically trained and prepared. To be there at all, one had to recognise this. To be a captain one had to accept all those risks on behalf of every individual onboard and take responsibility for ensuring they were recognised, handled, and overcome as well as possible—not by himself or herself, but by the management of the team onboard—their skills and knowledge.

This was not something Chris dwelt on. It was a given, accepted and understood from the very beginning of his life in the training ship. Sometimes though, at times like these perhaps, bits of prose, poetry, or thought would come back to him. Occasionally they were scary, but mainly comforting.

Some such were the words of certain hymns which were sung at evening prayers on the training ship—some just snippets of memory, from conversations or books.

> Abide with me
> For those in peril on the sea.

The Breton fisherman's prayer:

> Oh Lord, the sea is so big and my boat so small.

Robert Wace, a Norman poet in the time of King Henry the First:

> Very bold, very gallant was he
> who first built a ship
> and set sail down wind,
> seeking a country he didn't see,
> and a shore he didn't know.

Or,

> The man who enters the sea, on a journey,
> enters into great danger.
> This water must be greatly feared, for it is so
> horrible, lengthy and wide.

Over the next twelve hours, what Chris had forecast actually started to happen. The new swell shortened, increased in size, and gradually overcame the long, lazy undulations from the north-east. The wind had veered from its trade-wind-signature direction to come from a little south of east. On the first slam, the ship shook like a wet dog, and the bridge phone rang.

Chris had already spoken to the chief engineer, agreeing that they would remain in automatic bridge-control, but to be ready to reduce speed incrementally if and when it became necessary, so he knew it wouldn't be initiated by the engine room. He pulled back on the engine-control telegraph as the duty deck officer answered the phone.

'The doc, Captain—sounds a bit excited!' Chris took the handset, and Jonathan immediately said, 'Christ, Chris, what was that?'

'It's OK, Doc, just the newness wearing off!—no—she's pounding to a new swell pattern, and not riding it too well. We've just slowed down a bit, and we now have to find a combination of speed and direction with which she'll be more comfortable. How's the patient? Can you come up to the bridge for a bit? Then you can see for yourself and brief me at the same time.'

By the time Jonathan reached the bridge, the ship had reduced speed a little further. She was already riding easier with the swell right on the nose but riding up each slope and down the other side without slamming. At least they were still heading in the right direction.

'Well, his blood pressure is back to a reasonable level, and his pulse and colour are better, so as long as he's not losing too much blood internally, we should be able to start the lavage in a few hours. He's still bleeding, but it's fairly slow, and I think he's digesting most of it—otherwise he'd be puking, and we can't risk aggravating the tear, or whatever it is.'

'Mmm, rather you than me. I'll just look after *my* patient and nurse her along. If we can keep her this steady, will that be OK for what you've got to do?'

'If you call this steady!—yes, I think so. I'll be using soft rubber tubing, so there shouldn't be too much risk from the odd bump. I'll need a hand though, and not from that bloody chief steward of yours!'

'OK, I should be able to come down and help you—see how she's climbing the swells now? Our speed is sort of fitting in with the wavelength. Be OK until the wind shifts. The hurricane may turn towards us, and if it does, we'll be right in its path. We can't run out of the way as we're limited to staying like this for the moment, but she'll ride it out OK—just not going to be comfortable, especially for your patient. You need to get on with things if you can, while we're reasonably steady.'

 **CHAPTER 11**

GASTRIC LAVAGE

D ave looked pale and small in the steel-framed cot. He was conscious, frightened, and breathing fast. Having a strange doctor and his captain looking at him filled him with a mixture of gratitude and foreboding— it must be serious if they're going to all this trouble!

Chris took his hand and said, 'Dave, Doctor Jon is going to explain to you what needs to be done, so listen-up!' Dave nodded and breathed a big sigh. 'Go on then, Doc. It can't be worse than the old umbrella treatment!'

'OK, mate, you've got a tear—probably in a vein—in your stomach. I'm pretty sure your actual stomach is OK except that you've probably stripped out the lining, and we're going to have to be careful not to push through it. We're going to insert a tube down your throat, into your stomach, and then we're going to pump out anything that's in there— probably just blood, and then fill you up with ice-cold salt water.'

'Fucking seawater?' said Dave.

'No, pure saline—very strong and very cold. This should stop the vein from bleeding—seal it up—and then if you can stay calm and still, it'll gently heal up.'

'How can I stay calm and still with this bloody ship heaving around?'

Jonathan looked at Chris, who said, 'Well, as long as you're wedged nicely in that bunk and can't roll around, you should be OK, but I have to warn you that the weather is going to get worse, and we're in for a right old blow. Your timing just isn't great, what with a hurricane coming straight for us!'

'Oh, thanks, Cap! Reassure me, why don't you!'

'Well, you're going to be awake, and I don't want you to be surprised by anything—even the weather. We've both been at sea long enough to know that we can ride out a hurricane as long as we're careful—a tanker is probably the best ship to be in for that. We've got plenty of sea room, so if you do your job—keeping calm—and the doc does his, and I do mine, we'll all be OK.'

Jonathan had prepared all his equipment earlier while Dave drifted in and out of sleep. He had bags of saline in the ship's freezer, being kept cold but liquid. He had several soft silicone tubes, and a scary-looking clear-plastic instrument which was, in fact, a two-chamber hand pump which could suck or blow at the turn of a valve. The idea was to pump in a bit of saline, then suck out the stomach contents—then pump in more saline, and then after a few minutes pump out the saline again and replace it with more. Inspection of the spent saline would tell him if the bleeding was slowing down or had stopped. He had some gel with which to coat the tube, and an anaesthetic spray to help reduce Dave's gagging reflex from being a problem.

Chris left them and went up to the bridge where he was met by all the deck officers and the chief engineer. 'Just in, Captain—latest weather from Honolulu—looks bloody awful!' In fact, it was a weather report and a news bulletin, and it was worse than awful. It was catastrophic.

Hurricane Iniki had turned through almost ninety degrees. This was expected at some point because that is what such weather systems do—they track up from the equatorial regions on a roughly north-westerly course in the northern hemisphere—south-westerly in the southern hemisphere, and then turn through more or less ninety degrees via the direction of their appropriate pole. What is never precisely known is when this turn might take place, and therefore what the future storm path will be.

The good news was that Iniki was still over a thousand nautical miles ahead of them—albeit closing at thirty knots if they were managing five. A quick calculation suggested that they had around thirty-six hours before meeting. Of course, in that time the hurricane would probably reduce in ferocity as the sea temperature dropped and might even change course again. Right now, she was due to pass to the north-west of them, putting them in her dangerous semicircle.

What about the patient? How would he be in thirty-six hours? That was something Chris would have to discuss with Jonathan, but there wasn't much they could do about it 'We are where we are'—as wiser heads had once told him.

'Well, boys, we're certainly in for it, as we can't get out of her way, and we have to stay as steady as we can for a few hours anyway. I'll be in the sickbay, so adjust the course and speed a tad if the wind or swell changes direction. Otherwise just let me know if anything else is bothering you. OK?'

Chris went back down to the sickbay, where he found Jonathan ready to do his job, and a nervous Dave lying quite still, although his breathing was calm. Gently they propped him up on pillows, with more pillows either side of him and wedged inside the side rails of the cot. At this time, the ship was rising and falling around thirty feet, but fairly smoothly and regularly so they felt they could synchronise themselves with it.

'Open wide, Dave, I'm just going to spray your throat.' Dave started to gag straight away because Jonathan inserted two fingers into the back of his throat as he sprayed, and before Dave knew it, slid the lubricated silicone tube down into his stomach.

How d'you know it's down far enough?' asked Chris

'I measured the distance and marked the tube while you were away—look.' Just beside Dave's lips, the tube was marked with what looked like a ballpoint pen line. 'Up here for dancing!—or something like that,' said Jonathan.

The tube was obviously alien and uncomfortable, but Dave relaxed as the anaesthetic spray did its job, and they could see the tension go out of his neck muscles. 'Good man,' said Jonathan, and attached the pump to the end of the tube. 'Now this will feel a bit funny, but believe me, it's good for you!'

The colder-than-ice saline had been brought up from the freezer-flat, and Chris was primed to decant some of it into a measuring jug. He was ready too to take note of exactly how much went in, and how much came out, of the patient. A tube from the pump was placed into the jug and two hundred millilitres of saline drawn up. Jonathan then

73

activated two small taps on the pump, and gently depressed the plunger.

Dave reacted immediately, gagging and tensing up again. 'Steady sunshine—just a feeling—you'll soon get used to it!' Taps were turned again, and the pump plunger gently reversed. Brownish liquid—like diluted coffee grounds—flooded up the tube into a separate chamber on the pump and was then expelled down another tube into a waiting jug. 'How much in, how much out?' asked Jonathan

'A hundred and eighty in and just under the two hundred out,' replied Chris.

'OK, given a bit of blood and other things in the stomach, that's not too bad, so we'll go again to clear it.'

The whole procedure was carried out again with a similar result; then Jonathan said, 'We'll increase to two-fifty on the next round and leave it in there for five minutes.'

'OK, understood. How's he doing?'

'Seems quiet enough, aren't you Dave?' The only reply was a wild rolling of the eyes and a slight gag, which he managed to control as his eyes closed.

On the third go, with more saline, the return was two hundred and forty millilitres of brownish-pink fluid, with no coffee-grains. On the fourth, the colour of the liquid was undoubtedly lighter, so they decided to wait for fifteen minutes. Next time there was blood again, darker. 'Still bleeding, I think,' said Jonathan. 'OK, we're on the right track and doing him no harm. Let's do three more cycles with two-hundred, and five minutes retention each time—see how it looks then.'

This is what they did, and by the third go, the return was virtually clear. 'Right, now we'll wait fifteen and have another go.' This time they used 150 millilitres, and it came out clear. 'Got you, my beauty!' breathed Jonathan as he gently, quickly, and firmly withdrew the tube from Dave's body. Dave gagged slightly, breathed in and out hard before opening his eyes, tears streaming down his face. 'Thanks Doc, Cap,' he croaked.

'OK, my boy, now it's your turn—no sobbing, no gagging, no coughing, and definitely no aspirin. Just try to relax, even get a bit of sleep. I'll give you something to help you.' But before he could, Dave was away, snoring gently.

There were plenty of volunteers to keep an eye on Dave while the—by now exhausted—medical team had a bit of a rest. A quick schedule was drawn up to ensure that someone sat by him all the time, with a phone to the doctor and the captain. Meanwhile they went back to the bridge, where things were about the same, and then to Chris's day room, where they collapsed into armchairs, joined by the chief officer and the chief engineer.

'This hurricane, Iniki, if we continue towards Honolulu at our present speed, and she stays on her current track, we close with her at around 30 knots and will meet up with her tomorrow night. If the swell allows, we can change course a bit to get into the safe semicircle, but we're going to be in for a rough ride. We'd better just check through what needs to be done. Chief, you start,' said Chris to his senior engineer.

'We'll just bando everything up down below, press up any slack tanks that we can, like the boiler feed and fuel settling tanks, and lash everything down that's in danger of moving around. Short of that, we can't do anything much. Are you wanting to go back on diesel for the ride?' He was alluding to the fact that they had switched the main engine to burning light diesel—usually reserved for the generators—while manoeuvring to pick up the saline and the doctor. This ensured that the engine would respond to stopping and starting, changing speed, and so on, more reliably, but it was expensive, and they only had a limited supply.

'Well, as long as you're happy to run slow on heavy fuel for a good few hours, then I'm OK with that. We shouldn't need to manoeuvre except slight alterations in speed perhaps. Let's see how we go, but the last thing we'd need is a scavenge fire!'

'OK, we've got enough diesel, but we'll have to go into Honolulu for more if we burn too much. Would that be your plan anyway?'

'Mmm, too soon to say. If Dave's walking-wounded by then, we could land him and the doc outside the port and be on our way, but it all depends too on the state of the port. Kauai has been hit pretty hard, but I'm not sure about the other islands.

The report had said that Iniki had moved over Kauai, and on the afternoon of September 11, at 3:30 p.m. local time, the eye crossed the south coast, when its central pressure was approximately 945 millibars, and the estimated maximum sustained winds over land outside the eye were 145 mph, with gusts up to 175 mph, making her the most powerful hurricane to strike the Hawaiian Islands in recent history. By the time she had cleared the island, Kauai was in ruins.

'Ted, how about the deck side? What are your priorities?'

'Huh! My biggest concern is the doorway on the foc'sle storerooms—how some bloody marine architect could put the door to a huge space like that up on the foc'sle, on the forward end of the housing, I don't know!'

'Well, it was to do with the minimum distance allowed from the tank deck and the tank vents—for safety. Had to be on the forward end to get the distance, otherwise the design would never be accepted. The door has eight dogs on it and a padlock, so if they're all battened down it should be OK, shouldn't it?'

'Oh yes. Can't help thinking of the *Ranger* though. Bad weather knocked her dogs off, and they flooded the whole space—paint and rope stores, auxiliary pump room, and even pressed up the chain lockers for good measure—put her down by the head by three feet! Just negligent really.'

'OK, you know what to do. How about the chain lockers?'

'We'll get onto it straight away—re-cement the spurling pipes, double-lash the canvas covers, and so on, and put a couple of extra wire strops on the anchors. We don't want to have to send anyone forward in the middle of a hurricane, that's for sure. Oh, and another thing, we've been saving our empty chemical-drums—you know, the cleaning chemicals—they're lashed under the flying bridge. If one of them pops out of its stow, they'll all come loose and do God knows what damage. I'll get them holed and dumped overboard while it isn't too bad. Pity, really, the bo'sun was set to make five dollars apiece for them towards the beer fund! I'll get extra lashings on the lifeboats and bring the life rafts inboard too. Accommodation ladders are inboard anyway, so we'll generally lash and dog everything down, and that should do it.'

'OK, I'm sure the chief steward will check his stores and take the usual precautions—wet tablecloths, fiddles up, and so on—no, on second thoughts I'll remind him! Well, that about wraps it up.'

With the track of the hurricane turning farther to the east of north, it wasn't necessary to alter course by more than a few degrees to ensure that *Excelsior* would pass to the west of the storm track. This meant that she would be thrown out of the path, rather than into it, and that the winds might be a little more from astern once they were close. As Iniki got closer, the swell rose and drew more onto their port bow, while the wind increased as the barometer fell and moved towards an easterly direction, onto the port beam. Chris couldn't put wind and swell on opposite bows as the textbooks suggested, as this would have meant steering into the storm path, so he resigned himself to trying to find the most comfortable course and speed while still heading out of the path on the safer side. Meanwhile, though, it seemed like a seamanlike precaution to grab a couple of hours sleep.

Chris woke to find the ship's movement becoming more laboured. He went to the bridge for a look, having sent a message to the doctor asking him to join him, if he could.

With the wind now creating its own swell, which was in a different direction to the storm swell, *Excelsior* was finding it hard to synchronise with both. The third officer had played with altering course to starboard a little, but this hadn't helped. He hadn't wanted to go to port as this would have cut towards the storm path, and that was beyond his pay grade.

'OK, guys, we're going to have to go to port, split the swells. If we slow down a bit more, she'll ride easier, and the hurricane will pass ahead of us before we're too close—I hope!' As Baby Doc arrived on the bridge, he saw Chris at the controls, nudging the autopilot to port and easing back on the engine-control telegraph. With wind on the port bow and main swell on the starboard, *Excelsior* seemed easier, pitching and rolling but avoiding the trauma of two swells hitting her from the same side at the same time.

'What-ho, Doc. How's things?'

'Fairly quiet at the moment. Dave hasn't vomited, and he's calm. I gave him something to help him sleep a bit—a lot, in fact! So long as he avoids straining, we should be able to get some soft food into him soon—nothing like soft scrambled eggs in a hurricane!'

'That's good. Well done, mate. I think I'd rather have my job than yours! Can you see what's happening? Swells are rising, and as Iniki moves ahead of us, they'll change direction with the wind, and we'll just have to keep adjusting. Can you imagine what it must have been like in sailing ships?'

With a quick diagram, Chris outlined the pattern of the storm and their relative paths, showing Jonathan how things would change. 'Hopefully, we're not in too much of a hurry now, so we need to just nurse her along and wait for it to pass?'

'No, we're not,' said Jonathan. 'Dave seems stable, and, frankly, I'm happier here than I would be on *Arcturus*. A bit of a shy grin escaped his face as he said this.

'Oh, well, perhaps more about that later! We've not heard from her lately. She may not even go into Honolulu now—depends on the timing and the state of the port, I guess. Where was she going after that?'

'She's on the "Circle Pacific Cruise" from Sydney, so we were up in Japan, then across to Vancouver and San Francisco before heading back towards Hawaii—via you!—and Auckland, before arriving back in Sydney. I suppose they could miss out Honolulu altogether, as they bunkered in San Fran, and they can pick up more in Auckland.

Something about his tone suggested that Jonathan didn't really want to talk much more about *Arcturus*. That suited Chris, as he was glad of the company but happy to focus on his own ship and the job in hand. As a precaution, they had long been in hand-steering mode, with a man at the wheel rather than relying on the autopilot. With the wind and swell still rising, the auto was almost too sensitive—even at its optimum settings—and an experienced helmsman was able to feel her, and let her go, knowing that she'd come back without straining the steering gear with too much activity. Chris had also spoken to the chief engineer earlier about engaging both steering motors, which provided hydraulic pressure to turn the rudder. This was just for added safety, but it meant that they had needed to run up a second generator to provide enough power—using more precious diesel.

An hour or so later, Chris was surprised when Jonathan said softly: 'Have you ever thought that your job and mine are not that dissimilar! I've been watching you, or at least aware of you, nursing the ship along—almost as if you're feeling what she's feeling. You've altered the engine speed at least three times, and you're constantly adjusting the course just a bit to port, then to starboard.'

'Yes, well I'm trying to optimise our speed, and keep her balanced so we don't slam about too much.'

'It's almost spiritual, like a bond between you and the ship, working together—quite moving actually.' There have been times when I've had those sort of feelings with a patient—just nursing them along, managing their situation and getting them through the night, or the course of drugs or whatever. Pretty rare though—most of the time it's boring, repetitive, and more to do with geriatric hypochondria and people with too much time and money on their hands!'

'But it can't be like that in medicine generally, can it? Surely that's not what doctoring is all about? Why did you choose to go on a ship?'

'Ah, long story. How about I slip down and check on Dave, then get a bit of shut-eye and we'll get together later? Are you going to get a break, or is it "go on, stop on" for you?'

'Yeah, I was just thinking—I'll get Ted, the chief officer, to spell me for a couple of hours. OK, see you in my cabin in, say, two hours? I'm sure we can risk a medicinal whisky!'

Chris hadn't thought about it like that before, He did have a bond with his ship, and with the people under his care. He didn't dwell on it, but there were some $20 million worth of chemicals onboard as cargo, and the ship herself, of course—to say nothing of twenty-four people—twenty-five now including Baby Doc. While the ship was sound and the people competent, he did have the responsibility for all of them. That was pretty special, he realised, but spiritual? And did it make up for the long periods of bloody boredom, the bureaucracy, and the paperwork—and how about the separation from his family? Only this time before he left, his 4-year-old daughter had asked why he was 'going away again'.

'To earn some pennies,' he had said, at which point she had gone off and found her money box.

'Here, Daddy, have these—don't go away.'

'Oh, shit! Don't think about it—must be getting tired.'

He checked that Ted was OK to deputise for him and told the duty officer to gradually increase speed if the weather moderated. Then he went down to his cabin for an hour or so of sleep.

 **CHAPTER 12**

REMINISCENCE

L ater in the captain's day cabin, Chris and Jonathan sat sipping a very small whisky each. They both knew that things were fairly stable and under control in their own areas of responsibility.

'So, tell me about the *Arcturus* then, Baby Doc!'

'Well, I guess she's about average for her type these days—big ship with around two thousand passengers and six hundred crew. Spends her time cruising—either short trips around Europe and the Med, or long-haul with a world cruise every year, and a couple of circle-pacific trips. She's popular with the Aussies and the Americans, and particularly with the older passenger. They're the ones who've got the money and the time. In my dad's day the clientele was much younger, according to some of his stories—acres of young Aussie girls flooding over to Europe or taking a quick one or two-week trip around the islands from Sydney. According to Dad, they had only one thing on their minds, and it wasn't history or geography!'

'Is that what made you come to sea?' asked Chris.

'Well, Dad was at sea for a while. He never made command because he developed heart trouble, but he kept going on about it, to the extent that I completely resisted the idea. In his day, the main work in passenger-ships was long-haul, but Boeing 747s put paid to that, and the older ships weren't really designed for cruising. Loads of them were scrapped, and it took a few years before the shipowners realised there was money to be made investing in purpose-built pleasure palaces like *Arcturus*. He kept going on about his memories, and how it would be a wonderful profession for me, but I think he just wanted to relive it a bit, not realising that things had changed.

Anyway, I resisted his advice and got into med school after A-Levels. Quite enjoyed it to begin with, and I thought I'd found my vocation, but Chris, it gets you down—not so much the hours and the tiredness but the bloody bureaucracy of it all and the feeling that you're not really appreciated—so I started to think about buggering off to sea for a bit and seeing what my dad had been on about. There are plenty of new ships around, and they all need doctors onboard, so the companies seemed keen enough. Competition was tough though, as I think there are quite a few like me, looking for something more than NHS servitude!'

'And the acres of young women?'

'Never happened mate! Costa geriatrica mainly, but that's actually quite interesting. I think there's something cultural about all that. It's almost as if it's part of the way of life, or at least the expectation and the myth, that you step onboard a passenger ship and put on a uniform and then just screw yourself stupid! It's not actually like that at all. Well, perhaps it is for some, but the chances are few and far between, and I didn't really want it, if I'm honest—except that …'

He paused, and Chris said nothing.

'It's almost as if some people think it should be like that—that it's sort of expected—but perhaps it's a part of an ingrown culture left over from a different age, so you go looking for it and trying to make it happen, just because it's 'the done thing'. If you do meet somebody you either have a quick shag, which leaves you feeling a bit grubby, or you upset somebody who's really nice, and with whom you might have had a good relationship if you weren't in this hothouse.'

'So, what about your friend the nursing sister?'

'Oh, shit, well, there's a case in point. Sort of living the myth, but without much action with the passengers. Good-looking girl and a bit of a flu epidemic onboard—working together all hours and letting our hair down when we could! Seemed like a good idea, just for the voyage and a bit of fun for both of us. Can't you imagine? That uniform, pretty girl, months of cosy living with no strings attached—now it all seems to have got serious! My dad said there was always a rule: 'don't tamper with the ship's fittings!' Pretty crude and inappropriate, but maybe this is what he was on about?'

Chris didn't need to imagine it; he had lived the life. He remembered exactly when he had fallen out of love with passenger ships. During his early time at sea, he had been primarily on cargo vessels trading from Europe to either Australasia or the Far East, but halfway through his apprenticeship he had been appointed to a passenger ship, and this had seemed to be every young man's dream!

His main job had been to drive the big motorboats—'limousines'—at anchorage ports. Wearing his 'whites' he would ferry an endless stream of excited passengers ashore and back again, and among them would be scores of pretty girls who wanted to make eye contact when Mum and Dad weren't looking. Evenings at sea were spent dancing and meeting people in relative innocence, and the days were spent titillating the boats and generally staying out of the chief officer's way, so as to avoid any real work.

Later on, he would be appointed to passenger ships on a more permanent basis, at higher rank and with more responsibility, but being 'the Navigator' or making broadcasts saying, 'This is the Officer of the Watch' had its own allure—all leading to a gentle engorgement of the ego and a loss of any sense of reality, of 'real life'. The passengers were a mix of young and old, but everyone wanted to have a good time, and many seemed to drop their inhibitions as they walked up the gangway.

But this was fine—young and single, the ships cruising in European and Mediterranean waters during the northern summer and sailing out to Australasia for the 'Aussie cruising season'. Work hard and play hard—selling dreams and enjoying a relatively luxurious lifestyle.

'I've never seen an officer's cabin,' she said, as the gin and tonics were served by a white-clad steward. The other passengers went quiet, and some of them smiled knowingly as the beautiful young woman made prolonged eye contact with Chris, their host. The occasion was the 'captain's cocktail party'—an excruciating event at which all the officers lined up in the first class ballroom and, one by one, were introduced to a group of passengers who had been queuing impatiently to shake the captain's hand and to hear—first time for them!—his tired jokes. Ushering his group away and arranging for more drinks, even Chris was surprised at this full-frontal assault.

Her name was Georgina, Gina for short, and she was an air hostess travelling to Los Angeles to take up a senior position training staff for the new jumbo jets. She thought she'd go by sea and have a holiday before embarking on what she knew would be a busy and important job. A lack of assertiveness was not her weakness, and she skilfully took over as hostess to the group, charming everyone and giving Chris a welcome break—this being his fourth such party in two days.

As the event came to an end, she made it apparent that she'd like to continue her quest to see Chris's cabin—and anyway she was so attractive, and funny, and easy to like! So, she responded positively to an invitation for drinks before dinner the next evening. Chris then went to his table, where he hosted seven passengers for the meal before retiring to bed and getting a couple of hours sleep before going on watch at midnight.

Such a lifestyle was fairly routine; with two sittings for dinner in first class and two in tourist class, the more senior officers were expected to share themselves around and keep the people happy! Couple this with the cocktail parties and the inevitable cabin parties, and the risk of overindulgence was high, especially if the midnight-to-four watch was only a few hours away.

It often occurred to Chris that there was a sort of double standard—an unspoken 'make sure you carry out your social duties and keep the passengers happy—whatever that entails—but don't get caught or make an arse of yourself'!

In a master stroke of risk management, Chris invited his whole table for drinks before dinner the following evening, and again Gina was a delightful hostess—almost giving the impression that this small cabin was her home and that she wasn't just 'one of the guests' at all!

It got out of hand when Chris retired for his—now essential—pre-watch sleep. As he climbed into his bunk there was a gentle tap on the door, and in came Gina on the pretext of 'helping to clear up'. Chris's steward, Rosario, had already done that.

This was it really—a sort of clash, a cognitive dissonance between the red-blooded response of a young, single man to an obvious 'come-on', and a sense of personal and professional integrity coupled with a growing awareness of the need for a clear sense of purpose and pride in one's profession.

When he thought more about it, Chris realised that it was part of the culture, to which a blind eye was often turned. He knew people who said, 'I know the girl I'll have as soon as I see her walking up the gangway'—one officer who had purposely seduced a young woman who was on her honeymoon, just because he could! Parties, overindulgence with alcohol to a dangerous degree, and the drive to get notches on the bedpost just because—well, 'that's what we do—that's what it's all about!'

Well, who wouldn't? But if he thought further into the future—about any regular relationship, about marriage perhaps, and children and stability—would this be a reasonable way to earn a living? Would he be able to resist the temptations of that culture? Was 'selling dreams' enough?

After all, what did girls like Gina really want?—not him, really. Just a body and a bit of excitement to spice up the trip. So, what did that make him?

If he was honest with himself, Chris had had a problem with 'sex' until his early twenties. Being in the training ship hadn't been a good start; it was a hotbed of adolescent testosterone with nowhere to go, so most conversations were about women, and of the most lurid kind! Women were for one thing only, and if you didn't know what that was you made it up!

Then, just before his first trip his elder brother came back from a Far East voyage with 'a dose of the clap', a venereal disease not taken too seriously among many seafarers but dangerous nonetheless. Attempts to hide this fact from parents failed miserably when their mother found an appointment letter to 'the clinic' in his trouser pocket—she was sending them to the dry-cleaner.

What a time for Chris's first appointment letter to arrive! 'You have been appointed as a deck apprentice to the m.v. *Djakarta* bound for the Far East; please report onboard …'

So, her second son, all of 17 years old, was going to that same iniquitous area, where unspeakable women did unspeakable things to young men—for money! Thus began two weeks of constant nagging, threatening, begging, and exaggerating, which risked giving any young man a phobia for life!

Bangkok—the girls didn't wait for the gangway to go down—they came out in boats and climbed up mooring ropes which just 'happened' to be hanging over the side. An utterly beautiful girl, all of sixteen, attached herself to Chris and asked what she could do for him. After giving her all his laundry to wash, he gave her his canvas shoes to be whitened and locked himself in his cabin!

What was the fear? It certainly wasn't the risk of sin, or upsetting his mother, but it was the thought of a disease (some said to be fatal due to the American GI's overuse of prophylactic antibiotics). Also, later, in less risky

SOMETHING IN THE BLOOD

circumstances, it was the fear of getting someone pregnant—again one of his mother's absolute fears.

Well, condoms! How to … well, you know—just at the wrong moment, stop to put the damned thing on. And failure!—Perhaps the biggest fear of all and one which certainly didn't help the confidence or the necessary mechanics.

He did fondly remember a German girl though—a passenger some years older than himself—who gently showed him that these fears were unfounded and were blocking what should be a natural human life experience.

Everything crystallised for Chris when, a year or so later, he met someone in particular—she was a passenger on a cruise, but something was just different. For a start she seemed to recognise and understand what she saw going on around her, but she didn't lose sight of her own values. She was lovely, and affectionate, and she wanted to have fun—but not at the expense of her own self-respect or the feelings of other people. They didn't have a rampant fling, but they fell in love, and not just for the cruise. They eventually married, and she never asked him to leave passenger ships or the sea. He, however, realised that while his life—for the moment at least—was at sea, there were alternatives to carting people around for their own pleasure, or living an unreal and possibly damaging dream.

Chris didn't inflict these thoughts on his younger companion. 'Sounds as if this break with your routine is giving you a chance to think, maybe?'

'I tell you what, Chris, I was thinking today that I haven't enjoyed doctoring so much for a long time—and maybe it is giving me some space, and time for reflection. I'm as red-blooded as the next man and want to have some fun, but at one extreme it seems a bit cheap—no—a bit false, it just isn't real life. And at the other it's really rather boring—not real doctoring at all.'

Jonathan carried on musing out loud. 'I think I might go back ashore and get into trauma medicine—do a proper stint on A&E. They need people at consultant level in A&E, and I'm sure I could get that far at least.'

'Not staying at sea, then, or changing horses to become a deck officer?'

'I can't see myself staying at sea as a doctor, and I'm not going to start training for a whole new career, now am I? Anyway I couldn't do what you do! You're leading people, taking responsibility, full of technical knowledge, and you're connected by an umbilical to your ship!'

'Not so different to you, especially if you end up running a trauma team. I can't really see you as a country GP—not yet anyway!—but anyone can see you're a bloody good doctor and I don't think you've given yourself a chance yet. It's not for me to counsel you or advise you, but perhaps you've let your dad cast a bit of a shadow, even though you have gone your own way. Life is now; the things that appealed to your dad aren't necessarily there anymore, and they aren't necessarily for you.

'OK, what about you? Any wise insights into your life choices? Care to change places with me?'

Chris raised his hand and looked alert—his face had changed, and he leapt from his chair and was out of the door before Jonathan could say anything more. Jonathan then realised that the steady vibration of the main engine had changed to something more ragged, and that there was a different noise as something mechanical and high-pitched surged up and down with the movement of the ship.

On reaching the bridge, Chris heard the telephone ring. The duty officer listened carefully and turned to him— 'Scavenge fire number three cylinder!' he said. 'They've taken control of the main engine and are isolating the unit.'

'OK, tell the chief to call me when he can, but not to stop her under any circumstances unless things are really getting out of control—and to let me know before he does so!'

In a slow-speed marine diesel engine when burning heavy fuel-oil it is imperative for hot, dirty exhaust gases to be 'scavenged' out of the cylinders and replaced with fresh air, ready for the next compression stroke. The 'scavenge spaces' are where this happens, as the turbo-blowers force high-pressure air into each cylinder, scourging out the exhaust gases and replacing them with clean air. As the piston-heads rise and fall, oil, carbon or hot gas can bypass them, escaping down the sides of the piston into this scavenge space— especially if there are broken or loose-fitting piston rings on that unit. If there is a build-up of carbon or other debris inside the space, this can go on fire. The turbo-blowers, faced with the pressure of combusting material and possibly escaping exhaust gas, can begin to surge, further reducing overall efficiency. The problem can spread as heat and debris are transferred, so it's imperative to act quickly. Immediate slowing down of the engine is necessary, and the next step causes the engine to lose power and run ragged.

The chief engineer knew what was happening from outside his engine room. He had monitored the earlier slight reduction in engine speed and the inexorable pitch and roll of the ship. Though the movement was under control, he knew that any loss of main power and subsequent loss of steerage way would risk the ship turning beam-on to the swells, and that this would be dangerous—if not for the tanker, then certainly for the people onboard and definitely for the sick man.

His team were all there, and they knew what needed to be done. He said it anyway. 'OK, isolate number 3 unit fuel—cut it off. Increase lubrication to the unit. We've got control, so ease her down to the speed we were doing a couple of hours ago. They could steer then, so they should be OK now. We'll just watch the temperatures for a bit. No need for anything more drastic unless things go any more tits-up.'

The second and third engineers raced off to their various valves while the duty technicians gathered tool bags and cleaning rags in case they were needed. The chief phoned the bridge.

'Just the newness wearing off, Chris!' he said—reiterating an old standing joke to lighten the tension. 'Not sure I understand it—the unit was pulled in Panama, re-ringed and scavenges cleaned. Could be a faulty set of rings, I suppose, but we've isolated it and the surging has died down. I'd like to transfer the engine onto light diesel, despite our previous conversation. I don't think this slow running on heavy is helping under the circumstances.'

'OK, Colin, how does that leave us for diesel?—obviously OK as far as Honolulu at this speed?'

'Well, you tell me how far we've got to go, but as long as we're there within four days we'll be OK. And if it moderates, we can increase speed a bit.'

'Fine. Well, I'll be up here for a while. Say thanks to the lads and … well done mate!'

'Mmm, let's see how the temperatures go, but it looks OK—running smoother if a bit one-legged. A bit like a dicky heart, missing a beat each cycle. You go back to sleep now!'

Chris stayed around on the bridge for a bit—not because he needed to—the chief and third officers were fully competent, but he just wanted to watch and feel his charge as she limped into the next few mounds of Pacific water.

Down in the sickbay Jonathan was not having an easy time. Dave seemed to be recovering well and had eaten several small meals of soft, bland food. He was sleeping less and had been taken off all drugs, but his heart rate had rocketed and his blood pressure was up, and Jonathan was worried that he'd start to bleed again.

'Now what's up with you?' he asked his patient. 'I thought you were being good.'

'Shit, Doc, what's going on? I haven't heard any alarms, but something's wrong—I can feel it! If we have to stop in this, we'll turn turtle! I can't even crawl to a life raft, let alone fucking swim!'

'Dave, Dave, it's not going to come to that! The word on the street is that it's a scavenge fire, whatever that is, and that it's all under control. Tell you what—I'll get the captain or the chief mate to come down and brief you, but for God's sake, you've got to trust people.'

'I trust you, Doc—trust you with my life. Well, I already have, I think! And I trust the skipper and the others, but not this rust bucket. D'you know this is the third scavenge fire this trip?'

Jonathan gave him a shot of 'something nice to calm you down', and within minutes he was quieter, and soon drifted off to sleep. Jonathan climbed the four flights to the bridge, where he found the captain, all the deck officers, and the chief engineer.

'All OK with Dave, then?' Chris asked him.

'Bit of a panic attack—thought he was going to pop again for a bit!' It's a reaction, I think, to the trauma and the feeling of vulnerability—not helped by 'noises off' and the Alton Towers bit. He's calmer now and sleeping. I think he'll be OK. Maybe one of you could go down and reassure him in an hour or so? He seemed to think that these fires are a regular event?'

The chief engineer visibly bristled. 'Not on my tour they're not! Since the second and I joined last month we've cleaned all the scavenges and pulled two units. They were in a pretty poor state, mind—way behind on the maintenance schedule and a batch of shitty fuel onboard, I reckon.'

'Sorry, Chief,' said Jonathan, 'just repeating what he said—he was frightened—thought we were going to have to stop the engine and roll him out of his bunk'!

'Well, it might still happen, but I don't think so. The fire seems to be out—still a glow in the carbon perhaps. We're running reasonably well on eight cylinders and light diesel. Maybe I'll come down with you, Captain? You going to see him?'

'No, I don't want to alarm him. Ted, will you and the chief pop in later? If you tell him I'm asleep, he'll realise we're OK,' he said with a bit of a tongue-in-cheek look.

'Now, where were we?' asked Jonathan. 'You seemed to be sorting me out, but how about you? This is all a bit full-on isn't it?'

'Well, yes, perhaps it is, but there's always something either to deal with, or unknown, lurking around the corner— it sort of goes with the territory. Never boring, mind, but some trips are not … stimulating. I wouldn't go looking for trouble, but there are times when this job gives you— or perhaps just me—too much time for thinking. With a good team like now, I can go for weeks just monitoring, keeping a finger on the pulse, getting tired out doing pretty routine things—and standing on the bridge now and again while everything goes like clockwork. Sounds cushy, but it gives too much room for thoughts of a different lifestyle, or home, or perhaps self-doubt. And it's bloody lonely! OK, these people are good, and we're friends of a sort. We call each other 'Board of Trade acquaintances' as we're thrown together by the BOT who regulate us, and we may never see or hear of each other once we step down the gangway at the end of a trip. I can't let my hair down to anyone, cry on a shoulder, tell 'em I'm nervous or frightened! Can you imagine?—'Shit, the captain's scared—he can't hack it! What's going to happen?' Perhaps that's why it's nice to have someone like you onboard 'Oh, Doc, counsel me! Give me some advice; tell me what to do!'

They both laughed, but there was some truth in it which they both recognised.

'But would you give it up—try something else?'

'Not so easy is it? Imagine if someone said to you, 'Don't be a doctor anymore—go and do something else' when you had a mortgage and two kids at private school. Especially as a navigating officer or an executive captain— most people ashore don't recognise the skills involved or their transferability—even if they see past the parrot and the wooden leg!

'A superintendent's job comes up sometimes—less pay, working in London or some foreign port and even more paperwork. I must admit I'm sometimes tempted by the academic side—work at a Nautical College and become a professor, but I'm not sure I'm cut out for it.

'I did think I wanted to be a doctor as a youngster, and I've always wondered, but it's too late now, and somehow this week I think I prefer my job to yours!'

'OK, enough of this!' I'll get a meeting together, and we'll review how things are. Let's see if we can find out what your gin-palace has been doing in your absence too, shall we? Sparks has probably been tracking her traffic.'

The fully laden chemical tanker was very stable—all her tanks were around ninety-eight per cent full and not 'slopping around'. While most of the cargo was relatively light—solvents, alcohols, and so on—her centre of gravity was naturally low down, and her upper decks, while close to the water, were sound and tight. She was strongly built in Norway with a lot of stainless steel in her structure and good engines, and she complied with the myriad international regulations and inspection requirements. So, with prudent handling, *Excelsior* was the ideal vessel in which to ride out a hurricane if you had to. As the ship continued to make relatively safe, gradual progress, Iniki continued to track east of north, curving towards the east more and more as she did so. The farther north the hurricane got, the cooler the sea became and the less energy she was able to draw from it, so she gradually moderated to a storm and then petered out. She would never be forgotten though, especially on the island of Kauai.

While not comfortable, the situation onboard *Excelsior* was under control, and Chris was able to start making plans with his team—to gradually increase speed and head direct towards Honolulu.

'Well, Doc,' Sparks grinned through the doorway— 'd'you want the bad news or the bad news?' Jonathan's head jerked up as he came awake from his doze—'What?—what's happened?'

'Your floating hotel has missed out Honolulu and is proceeding to Auckland—and this is for you!' Sparks said as he handed Jonathan a telex.

The message was from his medical superintendent in London advising him that, as he had surmised, they were flying a replacement junior surgeon out to Auckland, and that he would be repatriated to UK from Honolulu. They felt that they couldn't forecast his progress accurately enough to risk him missing them again in New Zealand and suggested that perhaps he could keep an eye on his patient at the US Naval Hospital at Pearl Harbour, and then fly home with him when he was passed fit to travel.

'Holy Shit!' Jonathan could hardly believe it as a mixture of thoughts and feelings reeled through his mind. Not much leave accrued, no money saved, but hey!—a few days in Honolulu, some new clothing essentials (on the company of course!) and a trip home—have to be business class with a fragile patient, won't it? Wow! Even the delicate situation with Jenny sorted!—for the moment at least!

These were his first thoughts, and after a quick check on his patient, he went in search of the captain to get some idea of the immediate future.

On the bridge, a tired-looking Chris was in the process of again handing over to Ted, the chief officer, to keep a general watching brief while he got his head down. The officer of the watch was fully competent, but Ted would be awake, on call in his cabin if needed, so the captain could get some proper sleep. They had nursed the ship through the encounter with Iniki, and things were now stable. Best speed and a direct course for Honolulu had been resumed.

'Oh, hi, Jonathan! Good news or bad?' asked Chris.

'Well, good I think—haven't really processed it through yet. When d'you think we'll arrive?'

'Mmm, you tell me how the patient is, and I'll tell you what you want to know,' said Chris with not completely disguised irony.

'Oh, Christ—sorry! I did just go and check him, so I'm not completely self-centred! He's good—happy that things have calmed down, and he's eaten something today too. Blood pressure's good, and I'm happy with him.'

'OK, well, we'll be picking up the pilot at around 1600 local time tomorrow. We need to go in for some diesel and sort out the main engine, so we'll top up with fresh water too. I imagine we'll be in for the night. Now, I'm going for some shut-eye, so why don't we meet for a de-brief before dinner—say six o'clock? And you can tell me all about your plans for the rest of your life!'

Jonathan tried to collect his thoughts and drafted a message to send to the *Arcturus*. Easy enough to say to his boss that he was sorry not to be coming back and to update her and thank her and so on. Not so easy to know what to say to Jen. He decided to wait until he'd talked things over with Chris who—he now realised—he saw as a sort of, oh God, he almost said 'older brother!' No, semi-professional confidant perhaps? He recognised that perhaps for both of them, it was rather special to have someone 'other' around in an otherwise rather lonely place. Someone outside the structure, someone who wasn't prejudiced or judgmental—someone just to talk to!

Chris, meanwhile, had gone to his cabin and wearily jumped into the shower. And then something happened which surprised him—he felt completely and totally overwhelmed with a mixture of relief, elation, self-pity, and sadness; he started to cry—slowly at first and then quite uncontrollably, sobbing and shaking and heaving while the hot water cascaded all around him and eased muscles which he hadn't even realised were in tension, in his neck and shoulders and back. He went with it—something inside him knowing that it was good for him and that he needed the release. Gradually the emotions subsided, and he sat on the deck within the shower-tray, water still pouring, letting it all flow over him and out of him physically and metaphorically. Afterwards he thought he might feel a bit foolish, but he didn't. Just a sense of release and of self-knowledge—growth perhaps, of confidence, resolve and justifiable pride.

He towelled himself dry, lay down on his bunk, and slept for five hours.

Refreshed and feeling clean and tidy again, Chris checked that all was well and invited Jonathan to his cabin for six o'clock, before dinner. No whisky this time, but a cup of tea and a last chance to have a quiet chat with a—friend?—colleague?—non-judgmental counsellor? Perhaps all those things.

'So here we are—at the end or at the beginning?' It was as if both had asked the question although it was in fact the doctor.

'Well,' said Chris, 'for me it's somewhere in the middle—middle of my tour, but perhaps the beginning of a friendship? End of a particular incident but part of the ongoing nature of life at sea. More than that though, because you've really made me think about the nature of my job, and my skills. I've seen and heard something of your life and your work, but I've never had the sort of feedback that you've given me about mine. Nobody ever gives the 'old man' feedback. You have to glean it from the look on people's faces and the way they react. Head Office only tell you when you've done something wrong! It's really helped me to feel more at ease with myself—so perhaps it really is a beginning.'

Chris then told Jonathan about crying in the shower. His response was, 'Thank God for that! You're human, and you've got a safety valve. Maybe you'll survive without a complete breakdown! D'you think you'll go on doing this job until retirement though?'

'Well, I think I recognise that I do enjoy it—love it even—and as I've said before it's not that easy to change at my stage. I need to think a bit more about that though. There's a balance to be struck between 'doing' and 'being', and I've been 'doing' for quite a while, of necessity. In a couple of years when Imogen can go back to work maybe we can afford for me to come ashore, take a pay cut but have a more normal family life. Perhaps I'll look at the nautical colleges. There must be active roles teaching safety, management, emergency response, and so on. It'll have to be good though to compare with being your medical assistant and performing, what was it?—gastric lavage?—in the middle of a hurricane! One thing I know though. It's too late to become a doctor, and I think I made the right decision after all! What about you, Baby Doc?

'I think I've grown up a bit—no more Baby Doc for me! I realise that I love my work—just not all of it, so I need to focus on what I do love and buckle down to it. I'm going to look into the new NHS ideas about trauma centres—specialist units around the country staffed by the best consultants. I might even give more thought to being 'domestically settled'.

'Jen?'

'Oh God—well, yes, actually— perhaps. I mean, it hasn't started well from my side, but I'm starting to see things a bit differently. We get on really well, the sex is great, and I've actually been thinking about her a lot. I mean, I've not treated her badly to her face—just not been very committed because I didn't think I wanted the life that was on offer, kind of thing. Anyway, I haven't a clue how she'll feel about me by the time we see each other again. I'll contact her, see how the land lies and hopefully meet up when she gets home, so don't buy the new hat quite yet!'

The arrival itself was uneventful, but things were a bit more complicated than Jonathan had expected and even Chris was a bit bemused by the level of bureaucracy involved. He had taken all the necessary precautions of contacting the company's agent, applying for the appropriate permissions and so on, but of course there had never been any original intention of calling at a US port. By the time they arrived, US Immigration had decided that the ship could enter but that crew members without valid visas could not go ashore. The weather was calm, so there was no problem with rigging the overside accommodation ladder as required by the port authority, and despite a rather one-legged main engine and the port's insistence on an extra tug, berthing alongside was without incident. The pilot had boarded accompanied by an agent, Health and Immigration authorities, and a senior naval surgeon who was escorted straight to the sickbay.

Immigration arrangements had been made for the sick crewman, to take him off the ship on arrival into the care of US naval medical staff. His permits, visa, and such could be sorted out in due course, but what of his accompanying doctor?

Dave was 'walking wounded' by this time, although taking things very gently. Having conferred with Jonathan, the American surgeon had advised that Dave was safer waiting until the ship was alongside. They had been prepared to take him off by boat, secured to a stretcher—hence the request for the accommodation ladder, but this now seemed excessive if not actually stressful.

As so often, once the ship was alongside, everything seemed a bit anticlimactic for Chris. There was the routine stuff, of course, including obtaining permission to 'immobilise' the ship, and the Immigration issues to sort out, but the chief engineer and his team were looking after the bunkering and the chief officer had the freshwater in hand, so Chris said his goodbyes to Dave the patient and received his thanks—even walked him to the gangway with the hovering medics.

A very disgruntled Jonathan did not go to the hospital with his patient but had to remain onboard while the agent tried to arrange for him to fly home to England. This took longer than expected, so he ended up being escorted to an airport hotel—almost under armed guard—until, ticket in hand, he boarded a flight for home. It was all a bit of an anti-climax for him too, and not the sort of outcome he'd envisaged.

Chris had already said his goodbyes to Jonathan the evening before, and the baby doc, having seen the patient off the premises, had other things on his mind and seemed a bit preoccupied—'maybe it was something in the message the agent gave him?' Chris mused.

True to his word, the chief engineer and his team had managed to 'pull the unit', re-ring the piston head, clean the scavenge space, and reassemble the engine in good time. Eight hours later, full of fuel and water and with a very disgruntled crew, *Arcturus* gently departed in the predawn, and set her bow again towards Japan, where—with a bit of luck—the mail would be waiting for them, and they would continue the process of discharging, tank-cleaning, loading more cargo, and generally living and working together, as they had all chosen to do, for whatever individual reasons they had. For some, it was purgatory, for others simply a means to an end—nothing more—and for others it was a sort of vocation—something in the blood.

That night Chris was invited down to the officers' smoke room—he could have gone any time, but he liked to obey the traditional etiquette when he could. Two things he noticed: All off-duty members of the ship's company were there, and the whole room was decorated and illuminated by flashing orange lights and what looked suspiciously like orange drogue parachutes. People were obviously ready for a party!

POSTSCRIPT

Chris heard from Jonathan that he'd arrived home OK and that in due course he'd met up with Jen on *Excelsior*'s arrival back in Southampton. After that, things sort of drifted as they do between 'Board of Trade acquaintances' and they lost touch.

Time wasn't too kind to Chris, as he developed severe arthritis in his hips. He blamed it on all that rough weather and climbing ladders. He retired early, on a medical pension, and after two hip replacements and a period of study and redevelopment, he established himself as a management consultant. He'd realised that much of the knowledge and skill he'd learned at sea—particularly that to do with managing people and situations—was applicable to almost any organisation where people had to work together. He'd had to work hard to convince prospective clients that he, as a master mariner, had more to offer than seafaring yarns.

Still with an urge to travel, the family bought a camper van, and they spent a lot of time exploring Britain and France. One such adventure took them to Hadrian's Wall, and it was here that, with a fairly new right hip, Chris managed to dislocate the joint by stumbling and twisting at the same time.

With no signal on their mobile phones, Chris's wife, Imogen, had the presence of mind to dial 999. She'd heard somewhere that this would link to all service providers and might just make a connection, which it did! Within ten minutes a first responder arrived on the scene in his Land Rover, having found the car park adjacent to the main road nearby.

After a good shot of morphine and loads of gas and air, Chris stopped wailing and was able to ponder why his right leg was a good 30 centimetres shorter than his left, with his foot pointing the wrong way. Then an ambulance arrived with two further paramedics. Having promised Chris that he could keep the gas and air forever, and that he could have more morphine, they transported him to the ambulance where a decision was made to take him to the new trauma hospital near Newcastle.

Somewhere in his mind, Chris remembered that if you gave someone morphine, you had to write a big letter 'M' on their forehead. He'd done this several times—advised by the *Ship Captain's Medical Guide*—at sea, and at this precise moment it became extremely important to him. In fact, for the next thirty minutes it was all he talked about until they arrived at the centre.

This was like 'Space City'—a herringbone parking system for incoming ambulances, straight into an assessment area and from there to X-ray. After that it was a bit of a queue of trolleys until the patient was taken to a consulting room. All he was told was that 'you have dislocated your new hip, and a specialist will see you shortly.'

Chris must have dozed off, despite the bright lights and the noise. He was conscious of pain, but it was a 'happy pain', and he still wasn't sure if there was a big 'M' marked on his forehead.

'Right, Chris, the specialist is here, so you'll get sorted pretty quickly now.' At that he knew he was hallucinating because there, before him and dressed in the ubiquitous blue scrubs, was Jonathan!

'Good God! Chris! What on earth have you been doing to yourself, and where have you been?'

Gradually Chris realised that this was for real, and that, despite the years, he could clearly recognise Baby Doc all grown up. However, ever the professional, Jonathan immediately told Chris what the damage was and what they were going to do about it. There would be time for talking later.

'Simple dislocation, no tissue damage, so we'll give you a light anaesthetic and pop it back in!' That's all Chris remembered until he woke up with his legs the same length and all his toes pointing the same way. An hour or so later, Jonathan appeared at the bedside and, having checked him over and got him to walk around for a bit, pronounced Chris 'good to go'.

While Imogen took a taxi back to collect the camper van, there followed an intense period of catching up. This was one-sided as Chris needed to know everything about Jonathan's path, while his had been mostly predictable.

'I just think I grew up as a result of my time with you, Chris. I was sort of aware of it onboard, then more so later. Not immediately, of course, but it started there. I got home and was congratulated at Head Office and told that I was to be appointed to the new 'supership' building in Italy. She was to be employed in the US cruising market.

'All I could see was hordes of people with little wrong with them, the very occasional trauma, and a fairly monkish existence unless I developed a taste for much older women. Anyway, Jen wasn't going to be there—she'd had enough.

'I resigned! Took myself off for a few days and then started looking around for a bit of real doctoring. As I had thought, there was plenty of work in A&E, and this trend towards centralising services was really taking off. So … here I am!'

'And what about Jen, or anyone else, as I see you're wearing a wedding ring?'

'Aah, well, that was all part of the growing up! I had been playing at life, and I realised I was hurting people—Jen in particular. While that was no reason for making a commitment, it got me thinking seriously about what life is about.

'When I met up with her, I think she saw a change in me—after a bit of ice-breaking! So we decided to "give it six months" during which we'd see a lot of each other under more "normal" circumstances. She had a flat from before and was looking at a nursing job with a private agency nearby. I was able to locate fairly close and, as luck would have it, the city hospital was looking for A&E doctors.'

'So how did it go, this rather old-fashioned courting ritual?'

'It wasn't old-fashioned! It was normal, though it was totally countercultural compared to life at sea on passenger ships, or even the expectations of youngsters today! Anyway, after four months we were really in love. I moved in with Jen, and we got married the following year. Now we've got two children, Jen works part time, and we moved to Newcastle when a position came up here. How about you though?'

'Mmm, well, some of the observations you made really caused me to reflect, and over time I realised that the job I was doing really did give me everything I wanted, and that everything I thought might be missing was actually there, if I could only see it. I became a bit more aware and maybe a bit kinder to myself.

'But the industry was changing. There wasn't as much security, and I wasn't seeing much of my family. I couldn't say no to an appointment even if it decimated my leave period, because who knew if there would be another one?

'When the company doc said that I wasn't fit to be at sea, it was almost a relief, especially as I was still—just—on contract, and as sad as I was, I felt a huge sense of freedom, of being released from … I don't know what! Responsibility perhaps, or a debt to my father? Anyway, with the pension, it revolutionised our family life, and I actually got to know my kids before they grew up.'

Promising to keep in touch, soon it was time to go— Jonathan for a well-earned sleep before his next shift, and Chris for a very gentle trip home in the camper van. Two men whose lives had touched briefly but whose influence on each other had been profound, helpful, and rewarding.

ABOUT THE AUTHOR

Phillip Messinger was born in 1945, the second of three sons born to a farmer's daughter and a naval officer. After a private education in Loughton, Essex and three years in the training ship HMS "Worcester", he started his working life as a Navigating Officer in the Merchant Navy, going on to spend 24 years at sea including eight years as Captain of world-wide trading Chemical Tankers. He developed a parallel role in the Royal Naval Reserves where he attained the rank of Commander and the award of the Reserve Decoration & Bar. In 1984 he came ashore due to ill health and found work in Shipping Management, while gaining the qualification of Post-Graduate Diploma in Management Studies (DMS). He became self-employed in 1988 and broadened his field to develop a management consultancy business. Now retired, he lives with his wife Shirley in Hampshire, England, in close contact with his children and their beautiful families.

Printed in Great Britain
by Amazon